D0790459

INVITATION
TO ALL COUPLES IN LOVE

We, the citizens of Eternity, take great pleasure in inviting you to hold your wedding at the Powell Chapel.

Remember the legend: Those who exchange their vows in the chapel will remain together for the rest of their lives.

So let us help plan your special day. We've been making dreams come true for more than a hundred years.

Weddings, Inc.

Eternity, Massachusetts

Weddings, Inc.

Join us every month
in Eternity, Massachusetts...where love lasts forever.

If you miss any of these WEDDINGS, INC. stories, get in touch
with Harlequin Reader Service:

In the U.S.   In Canada

3010 Walden Avenue   P.O. Box 609
P.O. Box 1369   Fort Erie, Ontario
Buffalo, NY 14269-1369   L2A 5X3

WEDDING SONG

VICKI LEWIS THOMPSON

Harlequin Books

TORONTO • NEW YORK • LONDON
AMSTERDAM • PARIS • SYDNEY • HAMBURG
STOCKHOLM • ATHENS • TOKYO • MILAN
MADRID • WARSAW • BUDAPEST • AUCKLAND

If you purchased this book without a cover you should be aware that this book is stolen property. It was reported as "unsold and destroyed" to the publisher, and neither the author nor the publisher has received any payment for this "stripped book."

Vicki Lewis Thompson is acknowledged as the author of this work.

For my two favorite saxophone players,
Kenny G and Bill Clinton

ISBN 0-373-25602-7

WEDDING SONG

Copyright © 1994 by Harlequin Enterprises B.V.

All rights reserved. Except for use in any review, the reproduction or utilization of this work in whole or in part in any form by any electronic, mechanical or other means, now known or hereafter invented, including xerography, photocopying and recording, or in any information storage or retrieval system, is forbidden without the written permission of the publisher, Harlequin Enterprises Limited, 225 Duncan Mill Road, Don Mills, Ontario, Canada M3B 3K9.

All characters in this book have no existence outside the imagination of the author and have no relation whatsoever to anyone bearing the same name or names. They are not even distantly inspired by any individual known or unknown to the author, and all incidents are pure invention.

This edition published by arrangement with Harlequin Enterprises B. V.

® and TM are trademarks of the publisher. Trademarks indicated with ® are registered in the United States Patent and Trademark Office, the Canadian Trade Marks Office and in other countries.

Printed in U.S.A.

Weddings, Inc.
DIRECTORY

Your guide to the perfect Happily-Ever-After

BRIDAL CONSULTANT .... Bronwyn Powell

INVITATIONS & STATIONERY ..... Jennifer Thompson

ANTIQUES & GIFTS .... Patience Powell

HAIR SALON .... Dodie Gibson

CATERER .... Manuel Silva

BRIDAL GOWNS .... Emma Webster

FLORIST .... Julianna Van Bassen
                                                                Marguerite Van Bassen

LIMOS .... Daniel Murphy

FORMAL WEAR .... Ted Webster

RECEPTION/ACCOMMODATION... Lincoln Mathews

TRAVEL AGENCY .... Jacqui Bertrand

PHOTOGRAPHER .... Sarah Powell

LINGERIE, ETC. .... Christine Bowman

JEWELRY .... Marion Kent

BAKERY .... Lucy Franco

GIFTS .... Jean Stanford

FABRIC .... Marg Chisolm

SHOES .... David Guest

BAND .... Kerry Muldoon

Dear Reader,

Although I now live in Arizona, I'm a New Englander by birth and my Yankee roots run deep. In fact, one of my ancestors was hanged (mistakenly, I'm sure) as a witch. So I was delighted to write for the Weddings, Inc. series and help create the town of Eternity, Massachusetts.

As luck would have it, my aunt Bet invited me to stay at the family beach cottage on Long Island Sound during Fourth of July last summer. That clinched my decision to begin *Wedding Song* with a traditional New England Independence Day celebration, complete with a children's parade and fireworks over the water.

I had fun creating fireworks of a different kind between Kerry and Judd. I've always fantasized about becoming a singing sensation, so Kerry's dream made perfect sense to me. And I could hardly wait to zap Judd's big-city cynicism with a dose of the Eternity legend. Over the course of the story he learns to cherish the traditions binding the people of Eternity together. I believe you will, too.

Sincerely,

Vicki Lewis Thompson

1

WHITNEY HOUSTON said it all.

On Independence Day, Kerry Muldoon faced the ocean, planted her toes in the sand and belted out Whitney's "One Moment in Time."

As the early-morning fog swirled around her, she imagined that it was manufactured fog and she was singing on a stage before an audience of thousands. Because now fame was within reach. Her one moment in time was at hand. Today she would be discovered by Judd Roarke.

Kerry finished the song and bowed, accepting the polite applause of the surf, the bleating cheer of the foghorn and the encouraging calls of the gulls. "Thank you." She spoke into an imaginary microphone held in one hand and tossed back the cascade of dark hair the dampness had turned into a riot of curls.

She'd learned long ago that the northeast end of the beach outside of Eternity, Massachusetts, made a perfect rehearsal hall. The old lighthouse standing sentinel on a rocky promontory at the end of the strand was uninhabited, and early-morning joggers seemed to prefer the stretches closer to town. She could sing as loud as she wanted and practice whatever outrageous dance moves came to mind.

"You've been a wonderful audience," she announced to the sea birds wheeling in the air and skittering near the water's edge.

A flock of gulls skimmed over the waves, sailed in for a landing near her feet and immediately began squawking at her. She'd rehearsed here so many mornings they knew the routine. "Greedy, aren't you?" After pulling a crust of bread from the pocket of her shorts, she tossed pieces of it to the birds, who squabbled over the offering. Wondering how she should make her pitch to Judd Roarke, she watched as one large gray-and-white gull with an attitude hogged most of the crumbs.

Kerry cleared her throat and addressed the aggressive gull. "Mr. Roarke, sir—" the bird ruffled his feathers and stared at her "—I'd give anything for a contract with Lighthouse Records.... Well, not exactly *anything*." Now she spoke out of the side of her mouth to a sandpiper nearby. "You have to be careful with these crafty old goats."

The sandpiper cocked its head as if to question her evaluation.

"Okay, I haven't met him. But it so happens I'm giving piano lessons to his daughter, Rachel, who's up here for the summer with her grandparents. And I'll just bet he shipped her off for a couple of months so he could seduce some Manhattan mama."

The gull croaked and stalked away.

"Sorry. Didn't mean to offend you, Mr. Roarke, sir. I have no right to tell you how to live your life, I'm sure. But I do hope you plan to attend the Fourth of July concert this afternoon on Soldier's Green. Because I'm gonna knock your socks off."

Shoulders hunched, the gull glanced back.

"You don't believe it? Watch this!" She launched into "New York, New York," finishing with some suggestive bumps and grinds as she sang "It's up to you, Judd

Roarke, Judd Roarke!" She spiked one arm in the air, fingers spread, and spun around in a complete circle. She froze, then turned halfway back. Slowly. A man clad only in black nylon running shorts stood about twenty feet away, watching her.

As she met his gaze, he began to applaud with an easy measured rhythm. He was tall, easily six feet, with short dark hair, a nice build and evidence of a recent sunburn. She studied his chiseled features. She didn't recognize him, but the town was swarming with unfamiliar city people this weekend.

"Thanks for the show." He walked closer, his shoes crunching through the sand. "I didn't expect to get first-class entertainment with my morning run."

Kerry decided to brave it out. "And better yet, the performance was free."

He nodded. "I would say that's about the freest performance I've seen in a long time."

Kerry thought about her sexy hip movements and her unfettered breasts under her purple cropped top, but she refused to be intimidated. She lifted her chin. "I thought I was alone. Most joggers usually—"

"I tried closer to town yesterday. In honor of Independence Day I decided to be more . . . independent." He gave her a wry smile.

Kerry decided to learn the worst. With effort, she maintained her bravado. "How long have you been standing there?"

"Long enough to know you're going to hit up some old goat named Judd Roarke for a recording contract."

She flushed.

"Good luck getting it." He glanced at his watch. "Gotta go. I promised Rachel I'd bring cinnamon doughnuts home for breakfast." He turned and took off at a steady pace.

Rachel? Her breath caught. No, it couldn't be. Something that horrible wouldn't happen. Couldn't happen. She stared after him and watched the black nylon flap against his muscled thighs. He was probably just a guy with a wife named Rachel.

Except for one thing. Kerry's stomach began to churn. Rachel Roarke's favorite treat after a piano lesson was a cinnamon doughnut. Clutching her midsection, Kerry groaned and dropped to her knees. She'd just destroyed her one moment in time.

JUDD STOMPED the sand from his running shoes before walking into Stella and Allen Woodhouse's kitchen with a box of doughnuts. Rachel sat at the table, a bowl of cereal in front of her, while Stella scrambled eggs in a pan on the stove. Grandmother and granddaughter looked related, all right. Rachel was going to be tall, like Stella, and her features, even at nine, suggested the high cheekbones and aristocratic nose that made Stella a dignified beauty at fifty-seven.

Rachel's blue eyes sparkled when she saw the box in his hand. "Doughnuts! You remembered."

"Sure." He didn't admit he'd been so preoccupied he'd come almost all the way home before he remembered his promise and retraced his steps to the bakery. He put the box on the table, and Rachel reached for it eagerly. He watched her take a huge bite and roll her eyes in ecstasy. She looked so young and vital with her freckled nose and sun-streaked brown hair that his heart ached. He missed her like the devil, but this summer in Eternity was a good idea. And, contrary to what Kerry Muldoon might think, he hadn't shipped her off so he could seduce women. "I met your piano teacher today," he said.

Rachel glanced up, her mouth ringed with sugar and cinnamon. "Kerry?"

Stella turned. "Rachel, don't talk with your mouth full, sweetheart."

Judd waited for the smart-alecky response that had increasingly become part of Rachel's repertoire. It never came. Rachel obediently chewed and swallowed her food. Stella was a good influence on her—so good it gave him a moment of guilty unease. He pulled out a kitchen chair and sat down. "Your piano teacher has quite a voice. I don't remember your telling me that."

"I didn't?" Rachel took a swallow of milk.

"She wants to be a recording star."

"She does?"

"That's what she said." *And she also called me a crafty old goat,* he thought with amusement.

Stella turned down the heat under the eggs and took three plates from the cupboard. "I didn't know that, either, Judd. Although to my untrained ear she has the talent for it. She's singing with the Honeymooners, the band that's giving the concert this afternoon, so you'll have a chance to hear her."

Unless she chickens out, Judd thought. He'd acted on a devilish impulse when he'd dropped a broad hint about who he was. After the assumptions she'd made about him, she deserved to twist in the wind a while. "The Honeymooners?" he asked with a chuckle.

"Their main job is playing for all the wedding receptions we have in Eternity."

"Ah, yes. The Eternity legend."

"Don't scoff, Judd Roarke. Allen and I are living proof that weddings in the Powell chapel here in Eternity really take. Thirty-five years and counting."

"And I suppose you retired here to get a booster shot of romanticism?"

She made a face at him. "Go ahead and throw your big-city cynicism around. I'm thrilled the legend has been kept alive all these years. There *is* something magic about this place."

"I'll take your word for it." He winked at Rachel, who struggled, and finally succeeded, in winking back. As Rachel bit into another doughnut, his thoughts drifted back to the scene on the beach. Now *there* was magic. She'd handled Whitney Houston's song with a flair that could take her directly into mainstream popular music. Not too many singers challenged Whitney's standing these days, but Kerry just might have the voice and presence to do it.

He looked forward to seeing her perform again today, assuming she showed up. If she braved her embarrassment and appeared on stage knowing he'd be there, he'd have some valuable information about the character of Kerry Muldoon.

Intuition told him she'd be there. Or maybe he was the victim of wishful thinking. He reluctantly acknowledged she'd turned him on with her hip action at the end of the song. In fact, it was partly the picture of her in those white shorts, her firm bottom thrusting left and right as she sang, "It's up to you, Judd Roarke, Judd Roarke," that had caused him to walk blindly past the bakery on the way home.

"Daddy, want one?"

"Hm? One what, punkin?"

She gave an exaggerated sigh. "A *doughnut*. I asked you two times." She narrowed her blue eyes at him. "Were you thinking about work?"

He reached for the excuse rather than admit he'd been having lecherous thoughts about her piano teacher. "Yes."

"Daddy! You promised. No work this weekend."

"But what about your piano teacher? She's the one who apparently wants me to talk business." He knew how Rachel felt about Kerry. Rachel had given him a miniconcert herself last night and had proclaimed Kerry "the best piano teacher in the whole wide world."

Rachel scrutinized him. "Okay. You can talk business to Kerry, but that's it, Daddy. No making calls on your cellular phone, no looking at papers in your briefcase, no sending faxes from that machine in your car. This is a *holiday*."

"Whatever you say, punkin." Friday night Rachel had accosted him the moment he'd arrived and extracted that promise. He'd intended to get quite a bit of work done during the three days he was up here, but one look into Rachel's pleading eyes and he'd abandoned the idea. She was right; they hadn't seen each other in a month. He'd turned off the phone and left his briefcase in the trunk of the car.

Saturday they'd gone swimming and built a huge sand castle. Sunday they'd wandered through the Powell museum with its displays illustrating the town's history as an early seaport. At Stella's urging, they'd also visited the famous Powell chapel. Rachel had been as fascinated as Judd to learn that the tiny chapel on the old Powell family estate, which had been there since the midnineteenth century, had once been a stop on the underground railway before the Civil War. She'd talked for hours about what it must have been like for a slave to hide in the coffinlike boxes built under the pews, and Judd realized she was showing scholarly interests for the first time in her life.

Sunday night he'd played Monopoly with Rachel and her grandparents, and he'd even suppressed his characteristic urge to win. It had felt kind of good to shrug off the CEO mantle for a while and watch how his child was blossoming. Yet jealousy tinged his enjoyment, because she was blossoming so well without him.

Allen Woodhouse, coming down to breakfast whistling, interrupted Judd's thoughts. The balding sixty-two-year-old rumpled Rachel's hair and kissed Stella on the cheek. "How are my girls this Fourth of July morning?" He smiled at Judd. "Looks like you made a doughnut run for the cause."

"I understand some people have become addicted to them," Judd said with a teasing glance at Rachel.

"I *love* them," she said, rubbing her stomach. "I hope we can find a place in New York that makes them just like this, so I can have them when we go home."

Allen glanced down and Stella suddenly became very busy dishing food. She bustled over and put a platter of eggs and bacon on the table. "Rachel, the children's parade starts in an hour," she said as she poured coffee. "You'd better get into your outfit."

"Okay." Rachel carried her dishes to the sink and skipped out of the room. "I'll need help," she called over her shoulder.

Stella nodded. "I'll be up in a few minutes, as soon as I finish my coffee."

Judd looked at her. "That colonial dress you made for Rachel is wonderful. I'll bet it took hours of work."

"I loved doing it," Stella said, settling herself at the table. "She's my only grandchild, and the only one I'll ever have, too. It's been a joy having her here."

"Sure has," Allen agreed, blowing the surface of his coffee. "She's a ray of sunshine in this house."

"That's good," Judd said. "I was afraid she might be too much trouble, or too loud, or too—"

"Never," Stella said, her voice quivering slightly with emotion. "Never." She toyed with her eggs and glanced up. "Are you saying that because she's too much trouble for you in New York?"

"No, of course not." Rachel's recent tendency toward back talk worried him, though. He blamed the behavior on new friends his daughter had made in Manhattan, three girls who seemed to have lots of material possessions and little adult attention. The problem had magnified because his trusted housekeeper had moved to Arizona to be with her daughter, and her replacement wasn't as diligent about supervising Rachel. He'd about decided to look for someone else, instead of having the woman return in September as they'd arranged.

Stella hurried on. "Because you must realize we'd take her permanently in a minute. Now that we're both retired, we have more than enough time to spend with her."

Here it comes, Judd thought, the very thing he'd been afraid of. He tamped down his anger at Stella's implication that she and Allen had more to offer—time, expertise, patience—than he had. "I plan to keep her with me," he said gently. "I know that's what Steve and Michelle wanted."

"Yes," Allen said, "but they thought you'd be married by now."

"Maybe, but there wasn't any condition like that in the will," Judd continued firmly. He might as well take care of this problem now. "Rachel and I have made it just fine for seven years, and I'm sure we can—"

"But she's getting older," Stella interjected. "Don't you think a girl her age needs a woman around?"

Allen scooped up a forkful of eggs. "I'll testify to that. When Michelle was about eleven, she changed from my fishing buddy to somebody interested in eye shadow and designer jeans. I hollered for Stella and she took over. Kids are maturing even faster today, Judd. I don't envy you trying to deal with that metamorphosis by yourself."

Judd stared into his coffee. He couldn't argue that point with them. "I thought I'd be married by now, too," he confessed. "With my schedule it's tough to find time to date, and most of the women I meet are ambitious musicians on a career track. They aren't in the market for a husband and nine-year-old child, and even if they were, I know what their life-styles take out of them. I'm not convinced they'd be much help to Rachel."

Stella put her hand over Judd's. "For heaven's sake, I'm not advocating marriage just to provide a mother for Rachel. Far better for her to move up here with us and have you visit her on weekends when you can."

Judd's whole being rebelled at the thought. Besides, his brother hadn't wanted it. Judd remembered word-for-word Steve's speech on the subject. *Grandparents are fine as backups, but if something happens to Michelle and me, which it won't, I want someone from our generation to raise her. I want you, Judd, and whoever you've dragged to the altar by that time.* Except that Judd hadn't dragged anyone to the altar by the time

Steve and Michelle's boat had smashed against the rocks three weeks after Rachel's second birthday.

It hadn't seemed to matter then that he wasn't married. He might even have resented someone else caring for his newly adopted child. Ministering to Rachel had soothed his grief more than anything else could have. He and Rachel had bonded like two castaways, and the thought of giving her up to Michelle's parents, no matter how well they meant the gesture, sent cold chills through him.

"Grandma! I can't do these hooks!" Rachel called from the stairwell.

Judd turned to glance through the kitchen door and up the stairs. Rachel stood at the top railing, her dress askew, her hair in a tangle. Stella left the table to help her.

He sighed and picked up his coffee cup. If Stella hadn't been here, he could have fastened Rachel's dress and brushed her hair. But he couldn't have sewn the dress in the first place, and Rachel had boasted more than once that "Grandma made it for me." No doubt about it, Rachel's life would be enriched by having a woman in it who was more emotionally involved than a hired housekeeper. He'd just have to try harder to find someone they both could love, who was free to love them back.

2

KERRY HAD COUNTED on the children's parade, an annual Fourth of July event in Eternity, as a chance to take stock of Judd Roarke without being observed herself. If he hadn't known who she was, she easily could have hidden in the mass of humanity called the Muldoons. Each year at this time her whole family gathered to renew old traditions and ensure the next generation would someday do the same. Nobody missed a parade unless they were sick.

This year Kerry's three brothers and two sisters, all married, were contributing eleven children, two crepe-paper-decorated bikes, a wagon and countless red, white and blue balloons to the parade. Kerry's mother shepherded her grandchildren and their accoutrements to the beginning of the parade route at the school, while Kerry and the others staked out a position in front of the library on Sussex Street. The children would march from the school past Soldier's Green on Elm Street, circle the green at First, and finish up on Sussex before they disbanded for prizes and popsicles.

Nearly every building within Kerry's view, commercial and residential alike, boasted a decoration of flags or bunting. The draped cloth fluttered in a breeze scented with the tang of the ocean and the sweetness of mowed grass. The bandstand stood ready for the afternoon's concert, with hand trucks of folding chairs parked nearby. Kerry's stomach churned as she looked at the stage where she would perform this afternoon in front of Judd Roarke.

After the morning's incident on the beach, Kerry would have preferred to stay home from the parade. Rachel would march in it, and her father would probably show up to watch her. Kerry wanted to stay out of his way until this afternoon's concert in the hope that he'd have time to forget her rudeness and listen to her music objectively. Unfortunately her nieces and nephews would never forgive her if she missed the parade, so here she was, trying to be inconspicuous.

As the Muldoons laid claim to a section of sidewalk, Kerry urged the others to stand in front of her while she peered between them.

"Will you relax?" her sister Maureen asked, bouncing little Erin, who was too young to be in the parade, on her hip. "What you said wasn't that bad."

"You don't think calling him a crafty old goat could have a teensy effect on his opinion of me?"

Maureen laughed. "If he's that much of a stuffed shirt, you don't want a contract from his record company, anyway." Maureen, the oldest sibling in the Muldoon family, often made pronouncements like that.

"Yes, I do, Maureen," Kerry insisted patiently. "I'll never have a golden opportunity like this again."

Her brother Sean turned from his seat on the curb. "That's b.s., and you know it. Just keep sending out demo tapes. Somebody, maybe even better than Lighthouse Records, will snap you up." He lapsed into an elaborate brogue. "Sure, and don't be forgetting it's The Muldoon Gift you have, lass."

Kerry laughed and punched him on the shoulder. His confidence in her was nice, but he, along with the rest of her family, thought becoming a star was easy if you had the talent. Kerry was pleased they credited her with talent, but they didn't have a clue how many talented performers never made it. Contacts were everything in the music business—and so far she'd done her best to louse up the one she'd been handed on a silver platter.

Then, across the green on Elm Street, she saw him. She gripped Maureen's arm and stepped behind her.

"What? What?" Maureen asked, turning to frown at her. "Have you spied the great god Roarke? Is that why you're hiding like a rabbit?" She went up on tiptoe and craned her neck. "Where is he? Point him out. I want to see if he's wearing his halo today."

"Maureen, cut it out. I don't want him to see me here," she muttered.

"Why not? You'll be in full view at the concert this afternoon. What's the difference? Stand out here like a woman."

"Aw, Maureen, leave her alone," said Dan, the youngest brother, only a year older than Kerry. "Come over here, Ker. Susan and I will hide you, won't we, Sue?" He grinned at his eight-months-pregnant wife, who made a face at him.

"I think I see him." Shannon, Kerry's other sister, shaded her eyes and stared across the green. "The tall guy with the Woodhouses, right? Madras shirt, khaki chinos? He's pretty cute, Kerry. Doesn't look much like an old goat to me. What's the deal with his wife? Is he divorced or widowed?"

"Widowed," Kerry said. "Rachel told me her mom died a long time ago."

"A widower with a young child." Shannon sighed. "That's so romantic, Kerry."

"Maybe he's even available," Maureen said.

"Hey, yeah." Shannon stood on her tiptoes to get a better look. "What do you think, Sean? Is he husband material?"

"For crying out loud." Kerry felt heat building in her cheeks. "I should have known better than to try and fade into the woodwork with this family. Why don't you all shout and wave at him?"

"Okay." Sean stood up. "Hey, J—"

Kerry leapt on him from behind and clapped a hand over his mouth.

"Good, Ker," Dan observed. "Real inconspicuous."

Kerry slid from Sean's back and covered her face with both hands. "I'm doomed."

"That's what you think," Shannon said. "From what I can see, he's smiling. A nice smile, too."

"He thinks I'm a fool," Kerry moaned.

"A fool with The Gift," Sean said, putting his arm around her. "The famed Muldoon voice, passed down through the generations. Come on up here where you can see. The kids are coming. And there's old Louis Bertrand leading them, like he does every year. God, I love this place."

JUDD SPOTTED Kerry almost instantly, despite her attempt to hide behind her relatives. He guessed some were brothers and sisters, judging from the dark curly hair they had in common with Kerry. The whole bunch constituted just the kind of big boisterous family he'd always envied, having grown up with only one brother. He and Steve had even been deprived of aunts, uncles and cousins because both their parents were only children. Now his brother was gone. The family had winnowed down to Rachel as the sole representative of the next generation. Judd wished he could give her relatives by the score and family reunions that filled a place like Soldier's Green. He shook away the thought.

He watched Kerry's vain attempts to control her family's curiosity about him and smiled. Her ability to be embarrassed charmed him. He spent most of his time around seasoned performers who never turned a hair no matter whether they forgot lyrics or lost pieces of their costume on stage. They had to become unflappable to survive, but Judd always hated to watch the creation of the protective shell.

Then one of Kerry's brothers put his arm around her and drew her out into plain view. For a moment she resisted, but then she straightened her shoulders and stared across the green straight at him, her chin high. His heart contracted. He knew now that she had the courage to perform at the concert this afternoon. Was she building her shell even now?

KERRY PACED the open-air bandstand that had been assembled on Soldier's Green. The chairs had been set up in front of the bunting-draped platform, and a few people had begun to arrive, although the concert wouldn't begin for another thirty minutes. "I've never been this nervous before a performance, Grubby," Kerry muttered. "Never."

"Afraid of the crafty old goat, are you?" Elton Daniels, known to anyone who'd lived in Eternity more than a week as Grubby Daniels, grinned at Kerry. He still had the cherubic face that had prompted neighbors to offer him treats when he was a toddler. Finally his mother had hung a sign on him that read Don't Feed Me, but not before he'd acquired a nickname that had followed him into adulthood.

"I should never have told you what happened this morning," Kerry fumed.

"Didn't need to." He took his guitar from its case and plugged it into the amplifier. "It's all over town. By the way, can I have a new list of our bookings for the month?"

"You lost it again?"

"Afraid so." He gave her a winning smile. "That's why you're the booking agent for this outfit. I could never keep it straight." He winked and turned back to his task.

"You know, if I land this contract, somebody else will have to take on that job."

"I know, and I don't like to think about that, but we'll manage something, sunshine." The speakers whined as he adjusted the knobs on the amplifier. "Go test that front mike, would you?"

Kerry gathered the folds of her skirt in one hand and walked across the platform to the microphone. She, along with the rest of the band, was dressed in a period costume. She wasn't used to the layers of petticoats, the laced bodice and the delicate shawl around her shoulders, but the inconveniences of her outfit were nothing compared to her inner turmoil.

She wanted to run away, but that would leave her band without a lead singer, and she was too much of a professional to do that to them. She tapped on the mike and sang gently, "Yankee Doodle do or die, Yankee Doodle dandy."

Hank Anderson glanced up from his instrument and adjusted his tricornered hat. "That's the spirit, Kerry. Do or die. Knock 'em dead. Somebody like Judd Roarke wouldn't let a little thing like a personal insult stop him from making money. When he hears you sing, he'll also hear the sweet ring of the cash register, and he'll forget that remark about being an old goat." Hank was a high school English teacher by day, a keyboard- ist for the Honeymooners by night and on weekends.

Kerry moved away from the mike and groaned.

Ted Webster, who ran the tuxedo-rental shop in Eternity, played rhythm guitar. He came up to put his arm around her. "Look at it this way. You've already pulled about the worst stunt you could in front of this guy, so things can only get better."

Kerry shook her head. "That's where you're wrong. He can tell me I'm a no-talent excuse for a vocalist, which he might do just to get even."

Bill Northquist beat a little tattoo on the metal rim of his snare drum. "How about if we dedicate one of our numbers to him? How about working in that old Brenda Lee tune from the fifties, that one where she begs some guy to please accept her apology? How about that?"

"May all your clients have IRS audits." Kerry stuck out her tongue at him.

Bill grinned. "That little thing on your head, that mob cap or whatever, is falling off."

"Of course it is." Kerry reached up and pinned the white puffed cap more firmly to her dark curls. "Whose idea was it to wear these dumb costumes, anyway?"

"Yours," Grubby said. "I personally thought we'd look like Paul Revere and the Raiders, but you in- sisted, as I recall, and—"

"I like them." Ted lifted his guitar strap over his head and held the instrument like a musket against one shoulder while he struck a minuteman pose. "Ruthie says that tight breeches show off my manly charm."

Hank snorted. "Watch out or we might have to shoot you with that guitar."

"I have to admit Kerry looks like dynamite in that lace-up thingamajig," Grubby said. "If I were Judd Roarke I'd take one look at her cleavage and sign her right up."

"Grub's a sexist!" Bill challenged with a roll on the drums.

"Fifteen minutes to show time," Grubby reminded them. "And we're gonna be hot today, right?"

"Yes, sir, Grubby, sir!" chorused Bill, Hank and Ted as they snapped to attention and saluted.

"We're gonna give Kerry the smoothest backup she's ever had, right?"

"Yes, sir, Grubby, sir!"

Kerry smiled fondly. "Thanks, guys. You're the best."

"You just think that because you don't know any better," Bill said. "Wait'll you get to New York."

"Yeah." Ted hit a few experimental chords. "We'd better enjoy her adulation before she finds out we're really pond scum."

Kerry laughed, then took a deep breath. She felt a million times better, thanks to the efforts of her friends. She'd known Grubby and Ted all her life. Hank and Bill were relatively new to Eternity, but in the short time she'd shared gigs with them, she'd found them to be staunch allies in a crisis. "You know something? We really do look like Paul Revere and the Raiders."

"I told you," Grubby said.

"The thing is," Kerry admitted with a grin, "I liked Paul Revere and the Raiders when I was a little kid. And so did you, Grub. I can remember you running around singing at the top of—" She paused as she glimpsed a

tall man in the crowd. Her heart began hammering.
"Well, he's here."

JUDD'S ATTENTION was riveted on the bandstand with
its red, white and blue bunting. He hadn't realized how
much he'd been looking forward to seeing Kerry again
until he'd stepped onto Soldier's Green and she'd caught
his eye. His mouth had gone dry, and he was grateful
for the sunglasses that disguised his fascinated gaze. If
the shorts and skimpy top she'd worn this morning
epitomized one male fantasy, her outfit for the concert
certainly embodied another.

The material was the bright color of daffodils, but it
was the way the material draped her body that stirred
his lusty hormones. The skirt was full and billowing,
drawing attention to her small waist, and the tight
sleeves ended in swirls of white eyelet at her elbows.
Beneath a scooped neckline, the bodice laced firmly to
push her breasts up in a tantalizing feast for male eyes.

Then, to add the demure touch sure to drive every
man in the crowd wild, she'd thrown a gauzy white
shawl around her shoulders and secured it with some
sort of decorative pin. The thin material didn't hide
much, but he'd bet most men in the audience longed to
remove that tease of a shawl.

"There's Kerry!" Rachel said, tugging on his hand
and pointing.

There she was, indeed, he thought. Every time he'd
seen her today—on the beach, in the midst of her family, on the stage—she'd presented him with images he
was unlikely to forget. As a businessman he should be
rejoicing. If she had that charismatic effect on him,
chances were she could make Lighthouse Records a lot
of money. But he was reacting as a man, and that was

inconvenient. A budding recording artist wasn't the right woman to excite him, considering he needed a mother for Rachel.

"Come on, Daddy. Let's go over and say hi."

"Go ahead," Stella said from behind them. "Allen and I will save you some seats."

"Kerry's dressed up, too," Rachel observed as she and Judd made their way up the narrow aisle between the rows of folding chairs. "Doesn't she look beautiful?"

"She looks very nice," Judd said, issuing the understatement of the year. Kerry's dark hair beneath her saucy little cap hung in artful ringlets that looked both sophisticated and seductive. Styling hair was another thing women learned and passed on, he thought. Rachel was already complaining that he didn't know how to French-braid hers. Kerry would probably know how, he realized. For all that it mattered.

He watched her move around the stage with the rhythm of someone who'd studied music all her life. Her care not to look in their direction suggested she knew they were approaching and wanted to avoid the moment of confrontation as long as possible. She must be dying inside, he thought, and wished that he were someone else so she wouldn't have to be afraid of him.

As they drew closer he noticed that her cheeks were very pink and her breathing rapid. She was definitely paying for her unguarded comments this morning.

"Kerry!" Rachel called when they neared the stage. "Look at my dress!"

Kerry glanced in their direction, and inexpertly feigned surprise at seeing them. Her gaze flicked over him and she flushed a deeper pink. "What a beautiful dress, Rachel." Kerry smiled tightly as she walked, skirts swaying, to their side of the stage.

"My grandma made it for me," Rachel announced for the zillionth time.

Kerry leaned down for a closer look. "It's wonderful."

Judd swallowed hard as Kerry presented him with a gauze-covered view of paradise. The shawl was held together with a cameo brooch, he could see now. If she asked what he was staring at, he'd pretend an interest in antique jewelry.

She didn't, but she must have realized he was admiring her breasts, because she straightened quickly. To her credit, she looked directly at him, her color still high. "Hello, Mr. Roarke."

He had a good ear for nuances. Otherwise he might not have caught the quiver in her voice. She had courage. "I'm looking forward to my second concert of the day," he said, smiling. She had the greenest eyes he'd ever seen, and they were focused on him with such intensity his breathing quickened.

"I guess there's no point in being coy, Mr. Roarke," she said. "I'm hoping you'll forget my obnoxious comments of this morning and listen to this performance with an open mind."

Rachel gaped at her. "You were obnoxious?"

Kerry's smile trembled as she looked over at Rachel. "I'm afraid so." She turned her attention to Judd. "I apologize, Mr. Roarke. If we could forget this morning, I'd be very grateful."

Judd knew he'd never forget what Kerry looked like prancing on that beach. It would make a great album cover, although he'd rather not suggest it, would rather keep the image all to himself. Which was uncharacteristic and probably dangerous thinking for the CEO of a recording company. The Eternity magic must be fuzzing up his brain already.

"Daddy, what's all this apology stuff?" Rachel asked, tugging on his arm.

"Nothing." Judd glanced up at Kerry. "Whatever you said this morning has no bearing on whether you'll record on the Lighthouse label. If I allowed personal feelings to interfere with my business decisions, I wouldn't be fit to run a company."

"Of course I know you wouldn't do that!" She looked miserable. "I didn't mean to imply that you would. But I was hoping you and I could be fr—"

"Just sing for me, Kerry Muldoon." He didn't know if he could be her friend, not when every time he looked at her he thought of kissing those full lips and holding that ripe body. "Nothing matters but your performance. If you display the same level of talent this afternoon that you did this morning, then we need to talk."

She swallowed and seemed to gather her forces. "All right."

"I believe you threatened to knock my socks off."

A gleam in her eyes told him she'd accepted the challenge. "And I surely will, Mr. Roarke," she said with a hint of a brogue. "It's kind of you to give me the chance." With a nod of her head she returned to center stage.

Judd gazed after her. He hadn't been this attracted to a woman in years. Why now, with this woman, who longed for packed concert halls and a cramped tour bus? And she needed his help to do it. If this was some sort of cosmic joke, he wasn't laughing.

3

KERRY GAVE the performance of her life, imbuing the patriotic songs with a passion that would have made the founding fathers proud. The crowd responded as if attached by strings to the tips of her fingers. They sang along when she encouraged them, clapped in time to the music, even stood for the finale and linked arms to sway back and forth to "God Bless America."

Giddy with success, she warmly greeted everyone who swarmed onto the bandstand after the finale—Ted Webster's wife, Ruthie, Grubby's wife, Jo, and his two kids, Bill's very pregnant wife, and Hank's fiancée, Anne. Kerry's family formed a cheering section all by themselves and seemed determined to jostle their way onto the bandstand all at once.

After the Muldoons left, reminding Kerry where to meet them for the clambake that evening, June Powell, one of four elderly maiden aunts of the Powell family, clasped Kerry's elbow. "Where is he? Did he come to the concert?"

"Yes, Aunt June." Kerry had been instructed to call her that years ago, although they weren't related. Without June Powell, a tall woman with startling blue eyes, Kerry might not be on the bandstand today. Brent Powell, June's great-nephew, and Kerry had been friends since kindergarten. When Kerry's father died, leaving the Muldoons with serious money problems, June had stepped in and financed eleven-year-old Kerry's music lessons. Although June never mentioned her pivotal role in Kerry's life, Kerry felt deeply indebted for the help and was determined to make June's investment in her pay off.

"If he doesn't offer you a contract after a performance like that, he should have his head examined!" June announced in the overloud voice of someone starting to lose her hearing.

Kerry glanced around in alarm. "Be careful, Aunt June," she said. "He has a way of showing up when people are saying uncomplimentary things about him."

"Oh, you mean that business on the beach." June's blue eyes sparkled. "Brent told me about that before the concert."

Kerry looked heavenward. Grubby hadn't been kidding about the story being all over town. She should be used to a lack of privacy by now after growing up in a large family and living in a small town. It couldn't get much more claustrophobic than that.

"Serves that Roarke fellow right for eavesdropping, I say," June continued. "He'll sign you up, Kerry. I've had faith all along that you'd make us all proud. This is your chance."

"I hope so." Kerry searched the depleted audience for Rachel and Judd Roarke or the Woodhouses. She couldn't find them anywhere. Had he hated the concert? She tried to remember exactly what he'd said. Something about "needing to talk" if her performance matched the one this morning. She'd thought it had more than done that. She'd never pulled a better response from the audience in her entire career. So where was he?

"The word is he's a handsome rascal," June said. "Constance told me he was at the museum this weekend. I was upset with her for not calling me so I could get a look at him."

"He's . . . attractive." Kerry's spirits sank as the audience thinned to a few people and Judd was not among them. She'd been so sure he'd come up to the bandstand right after the performance. Maybe she hadn't done as well as she'd thought. Fear of failure curdled in her stomach.

"So where is he?" June asked again, jostling Kerry's elbow.

"Yeah, where is the great man?" Brent Powell echoed, coming up to put his arm around his great-aunt. "I thought I'd introduce him to Jacqui, see if I could scare up some business for her travel agency."

Kerry gave him an anxious look. She'd never been able to tell when Brent was kidding, even after knowing him for twenty years.

"Don't worry," he said with a laugh. "I wouldn't do that to you."

Kerry relaxed. "How was Disney World? I haven't had a chance to ask since you and Jacqui got back. I still can't believe you took the kids on your honeymoon."

"Well—" Brent paused for effect and grinned "—the kids saw the entire park. Jacqui and I . . . didn't."

Kerry laughed along with everyone else within earshot. Leave it to Brent to smoothly integrate his new roles of husband and father. She squeezed his arm. "I'm happy for you. And for Jacqui."

"Thanks. And seriously, once you're an insider with Lighthouse Records, I hope you'll keep Jacqui in mind. She'd be glad to make the travel arrangements for your tours."

"We're all going to profit big time," Ted added. "Bill's going to be her accountant, and I plan to rent you all tuxedos for her first concert at Lincoln Center. Hank's already started Kerry's tell-all unauthorized biography."

"Yeah, and so far it's pretty dull," Hank said. "I don't believe the woman's done one naughty thing in her life."

"Obviously I'm the only altruistic one who doesn't hope to gain anything," Grubby remarked, looking typically angelic.

"Bull," Hank said. "You want a job playing backup so you can kiss that insurance office goodbye. I heard you say that yesterday."

"Don't count your chickens, any of you," Kerry said glumly. "The big man was apparently so underwhelmed that he left the green without saying anything to me."

"I can't believe that," Bill said. "You were great. Besides, he heard you rehearse this morning and thought you were good."

Kerry could only imagine the worst. "I wasn't facing him then, and he couldn't really hear me with the surf and the foghorn and the gulls. Now that he's had a chance to get the face-forward version, he splits. Be honest, now. Does that sound good?"

"It's probably a power play," Ted suggested. "He wants to sign you for very little money, so he has to act disinterested."

"I'll bet Ted's right," Grubby said. "Don't let him intimidate you, Kerry. If he can hold out, so can you. Play it cool. If he starts talking about a contract, tell him you'll have to think about it, consult your manager."

"My what?"

"Yeah," Ted agreed. "Geoff Kent's a terrific lawyer. Tell him Geoff is your manager, and you have to run everything by him first. Might not be a bad idea, at that."

"Assuming he has the slightest intention of offering me a contract, which he probably doesn't."

Grubby took her by the shoulders. "Go home, take a shower and get ready for the clambake. Pretend you don't give a damn what this guy says or doesn't say to you. That's the way to handle these New York types."

"I can't go home. I have to help you guys pack up."

"Not today. You need a cool shower. Put on your tightest jeans and that spangly shirt with the shoulder pads, the one that makes you look like you don't take guff from anybody."

"And then *don't* take guff from anybody," Hank said.

Kerry gazed at her fellow band members, her childhood friend Brent and her beloved Aunt June. They'd been a wonderful support system. "If I make it to New York, I may have to take all of you with me in my suitcase."

Grubby gave her a shake. "What's this *if* stuff? Now go. We'll see you at the clambake."

"Okay. And thanks." She left the bandstand and started the short walk home. The skirts of her vintage-style dress swayed gently as she passed shops located in restored colonial homes, each decked out in patriotic colors, some flying Betsy Ross flags.

To get her mind off Judd Roarke, Kerry imagined herself back in the days of the Revolutionary War. She thought about the courage of the minutemen, the sacrifice of Nathan Hale, the valiant ride of Paul Revere. Her mother's side of the family boasted an ancestor who'd served under George Washington. If her forefathers hadn't been intimidated by King George and the might of the English army, why should she cower before the CEO of Lighthouse Records?

Kerry turned down the elm-shaded street where she lived and experienced a familiar rush of pleasure. She loved the restored colonial she rented from a family friend. The house was a pet project and the owner had furnished it with antiques. Kerry felt lucky he'd entrusted her to be his tenant. The sparkling white clapboard trimmed with slate blue shutters sat behind a white picket fence and a flower bed filled with purple pansies and yellow hyacinths. The house had no front porch, just a covered stoop. Kerry hesitated as she approached the house.

On that stoop sat Judd Roarke.

Aunt June was right. He *was* a handsome rascal, especially with that roguish grin playing across his face. She'd never seen that side of him, and she couldn't help but grin back. In each hand he held a tan sock.

So she *had* knocked his socks off. Unless she somehow mismanaged the next few minutes, he would probably offer her a contract. Spirits high, she unlatched the low gate and moved down the walk toward him. "I see you have a flair for the dramatic."

"It helps in this business." He slipped off his loafers, which she noticed were Gucci, and began putting his socks back on.

"I guess Rachel told you where I live."

"She did, but anyone could have, apparently. You're very well-known around here. Nice concert, Kerry."

"Thank you." Kerry watched as he pulled a sock over his heel and up his calf under the tan chinos. She'd seen those muscled calves before, and the tracery of dark hair on them, but this dressing in front of her seemed much more intimate somehow.

"You had everyone in the palm of your hand." He gathered the second sock.

Even you? "They were a great audience." She glanced down as he lifted his bare foot. Even his toes were sexy, she thought, before they disappeared inside the sock. She watched as he slipped his shoe back on and found herself studying his hands and his long, tapered fingers. Fingers designed for dexterity. She'd always been a fool for a man with supple fingers.

"Do you play an instrument, Mr. Roarke?" she asked softly.

"The name's Judd, and yes, I did, once upon a time." He glanced up, and his eyes were almost golden in the afternoon light. "Alto sax."

She'd always considered the saxophone a very sensuous instrument. She could easily imagine him playing it, his clever fingers manipulating the keys, his eyes closed in concentration as his mouth . . . But this was inappropriate, thinking such things about a man about to give her the most important business opportunity of her life. Still, she couldn't seem to help herself. "You don't play anymore?" she said.

He shook his head. "I was with a jazz band in college, but eventually I realized I wasn't good enough to make it professionally, so I decided to do the next best thing and work with musicians who could." He paused. "Like you."

Those final two words left her breathless. She stood in front of him, her heart pumping rapidly. She couldn't have said what excited her more—the power he held to make her dreams come true or the sexual stimulation he gave her senses.

"What now?" she asked, but the question came out in a throaty whisper that lit a fire in his tawny eyes.

"Maybe we should go inside."

She nodded and stepped around him, her skirts brushing his shoulder, her heart pounding. Of course nothing would happen inside her house. This was a business call, although suddenly it didn't feel that way to her.

As she fit the key into the lock, his voice came from close behind her. "Do you own this place?"

"No. I couldn't afford something like this."

"Someday you very well might."

Ah, so seductive, this talk of her future success. Maybe that was what had her so stirred up. She led the way into the whitewashed foyer, where she always kept fresh flowers on a narrow Shaker table.

On her left was the music room, dominated by an ebony grand piano on loan from Aunt June. On her right a living room held black walnut and cherry antiques worth more than Kerry liked to think about. Down the hall was a modernized kitchen, and up the stairs directly in front of them were three bedrooms and a bath. Throughout the house woven rag rugs made pools of color on gleaming pine floors, and snowy lace billowed in the breeze from open casement windows.

Judd glanced around. "Very nice. By the way, I didn't ask if you had a manager."

She'd totally forgotten to work that bit of information into the conversation, as Grubby and Ted has suggested. "As a matter of fact, I do. His name's Geoffrey Kent."

"Maybe you should call him."

Kerry thought fast. She couldn't imagine what Geoff would do if she thrust him unprepared into this situation. She'd seen him leaving Soldier's Green in the midst of an intense discussion with his wife, Marion, and he hadn't looked like a man who wanted to be bothered with business today. Besides, she was savoring the taste of danger in being alone with Judd. Such excitement didn't come often to a girl from the town of Eternity. "I'm sure we don't need him for our preliminary talks."

"You're not afraid I'll take advantage of you?"

She caught her breath. Afraid? No. From the moment she'd spied him on her front stoop, smiling that sexy smile, she'd decided to go along with whatever he proposed. Her pulse raced as she met his gaze. "Is that what you have in mind? Taking advantage?"

He paused a beat before answering. "No."

She noted his brief hesitation. He was aware of the sensual energy pulsing between them, but she didn't know if he was fighting the pull between them or fostering it. Perhaps this was how he wooed female artists to the Lighthouse label, by this subtle sexuality. If so, he had the technique down pat. She was caught.

She gestured to the living room. "Would you like to sit down?"

"It's really not necessary. This won't take long. What I really want to know is the level of your ambition."

She blinked. "I'm not sure what—"

"You have the raw talent and the basic training to be a good working artist. We have several people under contract like that. If they ever had ambitions to be more, they tabled them at some point and are content to make a living." He regarded her so intently a shiver skittered up her spine. "Is that what you want?"

Kerry looked into his eyes, mesmerized. "No."

His tone softened. "What do you want, Kerry Muldoon?"

You. The answer that popped into her mind jolted her. She'd never speak such a bold thing aloud and embarrass herself, but something about Judd awakened dark erotic yearnings she hadn't known she possessed. He was not like the men she saw every day in Eternity. He moved in a different world, and the excitement of that world clung to him like magic dust. "I want people to know my name. Lots of people," she murmured.

"You want fame."

"Yes."

He stepped closer. "I'll tell you the truth, Kerry. There are artists as beautiful as you."

She drank in the fact that he thought her beautiful.

"Many artists who have talent and training. But in order to have fame, you need one thing above all else."

Her breath came shallowly as she watched his sculpted lips move closer. He cupped her face in his hand, and she trembled at this first contact between them. She moistened her dry lips and saw desire flare in his eyes.

His tone was like warm syrup. "You need passion."

She forgot to breathe.

"Can you give me that?"

She swallowed. She would not turn away now. "Yes."

His gaze held hers for agonizing seconds. Then he released her and turned away. "Good," he said, his voice low and husky. "Then we have to get you to New York, try you in a few clubs, make a demo in our studios. If all that goes well, we can start talking about a contract."

Kerry stood in a dazed stupor. She'd been certain he was about to kiss her, but then he'd broken the spell, denied himself the gesture. Was he attracted to her, yet considered it inappropriate? She would have kissed him back, which was probably also inappropriate. She didn't know this world. She'd better be careful.

He rubbed the back of his neck. "Can you get away from your responsibilities for a couple of weeks?"

She forced her brain to work. Getting away wouldn't be easy. Her piano students were a dedicated bunch, and most had opted to continue lessons through the summer. She'd booked the band for several performances, and Lord knew who would handle future bookings while she was gone. Then there was the obligation to the First Congregational church choir, which she led. "I . . . yes, of course . . . somehow." Then she thought of another obstacle. "I don't have a lot of money saved, and I know New York's expensive, so I'm not sure—"

"Lighthouse Records will handle travel expenses, accommodation and food as our initial investment in you. All we need from you now is your time." He turned back to her and his expression was guarded, businesslike. "Can you do it? Within the next week?"

Kerry felt dizzy from the energy coursing between them and the abrupt need to decide her future, but somehow she managed to say she could.

"All right." He pulled out his wallet. "Let me know when you'll arrive." He handed her his business card.

She took the card without looking at it. She felt as if she were poised in the last car of a roller coaster just before it took a steep drop.

He started toward the door and turned back. "I have another question. It's personal, so you don't have to answer if you don't want to."

"What is it?"

"This may sound cold and calculating to you, but it helps when you're launching a career if you've got no ties, no boyfriends to distract you from your work. Any men in your life?"

Kerry thought of her lackluster love life. Hank was right; she hadn't done anything that would spice up an unauthorized biography. She'd poured most of her vitality into her music, and the two men she'd dated seriously hadn't approved of that, so she'd eventually parted from them with little regret. Someone like Judd would understand and approve of an ambitious woman, she thought fleetingly. "No one."

His golden eyes burned for a second. "Then the men in Eternity must be total fools." He turned and walked out the door.

4

STELLA INFORMED Judd that the annual clambake on the beach before the fireworks was the biggest fund-raiser of the year for the Eternity Women's Preservation Society.

"Does the money go toward preserving Eternity's women?" he asked with a grin as she sprayed everyone with mosquito repellent before they set off for the clambake.

"It goes toward preserving us from bad jokes," Stella said, giving him an extra dousing of spray that made him cough and Rachel giggle.

Despite his kidding, Judd wouldn't have missed the event. Kerry would be there, and no matter how many times he warned himself to stay away from her, especially after the close call that afternoon, he couldn't do it. Tonight would be safe, because the whole town would be their chaperons.

In New York he'd assign somebody else to shepherd her through the auditioning steps. But in the meantime, he wanted to see her once more against the backdrop of the ocean that seemed so much a part of her. Her music videos should be done here in Eternity, of course. The place was a natural, and so was she.

He accepted the picnic blanket and wicker basket of plates and utensils Stella handed him, and followed everyone out to Allen's car. He couldn't remember the last time he'd been to a picnic on a beach. The blanket and hamper filled him with nostalgia, and if he hadn't had Rachel skipping at his side chattering about the fireworks, he'd have imagined he was twenty again, heading out with his brother, Steve, and their respective girlfriends for a bonfire and hot-dog roast in the sand.

He and Steve had grown up on the West Coast, north of L.A., and, once they'd reached adulthood, by mutual agreement had put a continent between them and their successful, overbearing parents. He tried to imagine his mother and father making a bid to have Rachel live with them, and couldn't. Both film agents, they'd barely had time for their own children, let alone a grandchild. They sent elaborate presents and demanded current pictures they could pass around, but that about covered their involvement.

Allen Woodhouse maneuvered the car along the narrow road to the beach, which wound through marshes teeming with wildlife, the same road Judd had taken on foot that morning.

Stella gestured off to their right across the salt marsh. "To give you a proper reply to that smart-alecky remark you made earlier, Judd, the profit from this clambake will help buy those woods from the Seatham Corporation, so we can keep that area natural."

"Sounds like a good cause."

"There's a real ruckus about it going on, let me tell you. Geoffrey Kent is on one side of the issue and his wife, Marion, is leading the opposition."

Judd tried to remember where he'd heard of Geoffrey Kent and finally remembered Kerry had named him as her manager. "How is Geoffrey Kent involved?"

"He's a lawyer who's been hired by Seatham to push the land purchase and condo construction. Marion's on the Conservation Commission, which is dead set against the development. Some people are wondering if they'll divorce over it."

So Kerry had herself a lawyer as a manager. Good move. "What do you think?" he asked.

"I don't think they'll divorce." Stella turned in her seat and gave him a smug smile. "They were married in the Powell chapel, you see."

Allen snorted. "You walked right into that one, Judd."

"Allen, you believe in the legend just as much as I do," Stella scolded. "Oh, Rachel, there's an osprey perched on that dead tree over there. See it?"

"Yeah! Neat, Grandma! That makes six times I've seen one so far this summer. Look, Dad, right over there."

"Pretty impressive." Judd recalled that Rachel loved watching wildlife specials on TV, probably because her personal exposure to wildlife was limited to the zoo, pigeons on the windowsill of their apartment and ducks on the lake in Central Park. Was that too much of a hothouse existence for a growing child? Here in Eternity she played outside most of the time and seemed to have forgotten completely about television.

In a short time they were searching for a parking space in the packed lot adjoining the beach. After Allen nabbed one, Judd helped unload the car and followed Rachel and the Woodhouses across the slatted walkway over the dunes. Once there he searched the milling crowd on the beach for Kerry. She wasn't hard to spot, decked out in a glittery white blouse and snug jeans. Nestled into a cluster of family members, she shone for him like a diamond in its setting.

He waved when she caught his eye, and she waved back, but she didn't come over. Just as well, he thought. Maybe he'd scared her this afternoon, but he didn't think so. Unless his instincts were shot she'd been with him all the way. Fortunately he'd found some control at the last minute. Starting something with Kerry, no matter how much she attracted him, would be a big mistake.

Stella and Allen spread a blanket in the sand, and Judd followed Rachel's lead, taking off his shoes and socks. He remembered his stunt with the socks that afternoon with Kerry and felt a new surge of desire. She'd looked so damned good, coming up that walk with anticipation glowing on her cheeks.

"Judd?" Stella jostled his arm. "Ready to get some food?"

He snapped out of his reverie. He had to stop this kind of daydreaming, and he would, once he escaped the seductive atmosphere of this town. Fanciful costumes during the day, a romantic beach party at night— no wonder he was acting like an idiot. New York would bring him back to reality—it always did.

Stella directed them to the buffet line at the folding tables set up on the beach. The aroma of seafood and roasted corn mingled with the salt air in a heady combination that Judd thought rivaled some of the better restaurants in New York. But again, it was probably the unfamiliar surroundings.

"So you're Rachel's dad."

Judd turned toward the woman behind him in line. She had a pleasant face, although a little too heavily made-up for his tastes, and hair tinted a shade between burgundy and rosé wine. "I'm Rachel's dad," he confirmed. "And you're . . . ?"

"Dodie Gibson." She thrust out her hand. "I do Stella's hair, and she brought Rachel in for a cut soon after she got here. Wonderful little girl."

"Yes, she is."

Dodie glanced around impatiently. "I was supposed to have a date for this shindig, but I think I've been stood up. You aren't attached to anyone, are you, Mr. Roarke?"

"Uh—"

"We could just eat together, you know? I hate to eat alone, don't you?"

"Well, I'm here with Rachel and the Woodhouses, so—"

"That's great!" Dodie's earrings, a pair of brilliant toucans, jingled. "We're good friends." She stood on tiptoe. "Stella!" When Stella turned, Dodie smiled. "I just invited myself to share your picnic blanket. Is that okay?"

"That's fine, Dodie."

Judd heard amused forebearance in Stella's reply. As Dodie began to chatter to him about the lovely evening and the excellent food, she found excuses to lay her hand on his arm or to brush against him. Well, here was a woman obviously in the market, he thought. And she'd be able to French-braid Rachel's hair.

Judd thought about the possibility of Dodie Gibson for about two seconds before his gaze wandered over to Kerry. She sat on a blanket holding a toddler in her lap and laughing as the baby patted the spangles on her shirt. Judd remembered Steve's saying he'd known Michelle was the woman for him the first moment he saw her. Steve's words echoed in Judd's mind as he watched Kerry.

"And by the way, Judd . . . May I call you Judd?"

He brought his attention back to Dodie, who was looking at him with complete absorption. "Sure. But, Dodie, I should warn you that—"

"Don't bother warning me." She flashed him a bright smile. "I've been married five times, and warnings never did work with me. Here, take a plate."

He accepted the plate she gave him, let her load it up with food and walked between Dodie and Rachel as they headed for the blanket. Rachel rolled her eyes at him when he glanced down at her. He tried not to laugh. He and Rachel had been through this enough times that she could sense when her father wasn't interested in a woman's advances.

He savored the fresh clams and sweet corn as Dodie monopolized the conversation. She was funny, and soon had everyone laughing at the stories she told about the beauty shop and her numerous husbands.

"Why all the marriages, Dodie?" he asked finally. "I thought Eternity was dedicated to the one man, one woman concept."

"So far I've never been able to talk any guy into getting married in the Powell chapel," Dodie explained. "Which tells you how committed they were, huh?" She laughed. "How do you stand on the legend, Judd?"

"I'm a New Yorker. We're not famous for our sentimentality."

"You should spend more time in Eternity," Dodie said. "We'd fix that."

"Could be." Throughout their conversation he'd subtly kept track of Kerry. As she moved through the gathering on the beach the crowd reacted to her as if she

were a princess. Everyone seemed to love her. That sort
of charisma was a good sign for her future fame, although she'd eventually have to give up such intimate
communication with her fans. Kerry had a lot to learn,
but he had realized today he was the last person in the
world who should teach her.

His speech about passion had not gone well. It was
a good speech, one he'd used before with hopefuls to
clarify what their ambitions were. But his attraction to
Kerry had given it a whole new direction. The concept
of an untapped well of passion in Kerry Muldoon fascinated him.

And then he'd worked in that question about her love
life, which he'd never asked another artist before signing them to a contract. The question wasn't totally out
of left field—a love relationship could get in the way of
a budding career. But it was all a rationalization, because his motivation for asking hadn't had anything to
do with Kerry's professional future. He'd wanted to
know as a man. A man dazzled by this little town and
its reigning princess, Kerry Muldoon.

"Daddy, pass the salt, please." Rachel nudged him,
and he realized he'd zoned out again.

"Sure thing." He reached for the shaker sitting beside him on the blanket and passed it to Rachel with a
smile. Her mouth glistened with the butter she'd spread
on her corn. She'd skipped the clams, but he could see
from the mangled cobs on her plate that she'd sampled
liberal amounts of the tender white New England corn.

"We have to come back here every single Fourth of
July," Rachel announced. "Okay, Daddy?"

"Okay." He tried to picture this town without Kerry
in it, which would be the case next summer if she suc-

ceeded the way he thought she might. The thought depressed him.

"But, Rachel, weren't we going to talk to your father about your spending the whole summer with us from now on?" her grandmother said, looking up from her plate of clams.

"Yeah," Rachel said slowly, casting a sideways glance at her father. "We were."

Every summer, Judd thought. No more summers with Rachel. Three months of every year chopped out of his life with her.

"But I think Daddy gets lonesome in New York," Rachel added, chomping down on her corn.

"I'm okay, punkin," he said quickly. God forbid she'd stay home with him out of pity.

"Then you don't miss me?" Her blue gaze was accusing.

He laughed. "You've got me in a no-win situation. Either I admit to missing you and then you stay home for the sake of old Dad, or I don't miss you and then you think I don't care."

"Which is it?" she asked with the persistence of a nine-year-old.

"Neither." He reached out and smoothed her hair.

"Daddy! You'll mess up Grandma's braiding job."

"Sorry." He removed his hand. "What I mean is, I miss you, but I want you to stay here during the summers, just like you planned, with Grandma and Grandpa, if that's what you want. I think it's great you can get out of the city for a few months. I wish I could." Now where had that come from? He'd never thought that before.

Dodie leapt on the statement. "Then why don't you?" She pried open another clam. "I hear about executives all the time who keep in touch with their offices by telephone and fax machines. You could make Eternity your home base for the summer."

The idea sounded preposterous to Judd, but he didn't say so. No one sitting on the blanket could imagine the responsibilities he shouldered as founder and CEO of Lighthouse Records. He had a dedicated staff, and the other officers of the company worked hard, but nobody could be expected to care the way he did.

"You should really consider moving your operation up here for the summer," Stella urged. "We have the space. You could turn that bedroom you use into an office with no trouble at all."

"I'd build some shelves, cabinets, anything you want," Allen said.

"That's very generous of you both." Judd glanced at Rachel. Her expression told him she knew he wouldn't consider it. But he hoped that someday she'd consider joining the business, and that eventually she'd take it over. He wanted to shepherd the company carefully until then.

Besides, this town seemed to have the capacity to eat his brain. No telling what sort of softheaded business decisions he'd make if he based his operation here in the land of love and everlasting marriages.

"Unfortunately," he began, "I need to have more than phone and fax communication with my office. I need to be there in person, be able to read people's faces when they discuss deals with me. It's a tricky business. Plus, when I'm in New York I can check out the talent in the clubs more easily. That's where we've discovered some of our big names, as I guess you know."

"I suppose you do need to stay in the thick of things," Stella said. "And you work with so many important people it might be boring staying down here for the summer."

From the corner of his eye Judd could see Kerry strumming a guitar while she sat surrounded by friends and family. Soft light from the setting sun tinged her face and sparkled in her eyes. "Not necessarily boring," he said. "Maybe 'inconvenient' is a better word."

"I'm still impressed you got that autographed album for me from Julio Iglesias."

"If he wouldn't sign with us, the least he could do was give me an autographed album for my daughter's grandmother," Judd said with a smile.

"Julio Iglesias?" Dodie gaped. "You *know* him?"

"He knows tons of people," Rachel said with a wave of her hand. "Bruce Springsteen comes over all the time, and we go for pizza sometimes with Cyndi Lauper."

Dodie's mouth gaped open. "You told me about going out for pizza with somebody named Cyndi when I trimmed your hair, but I thought Cyndi was one of your little friends."

"Well, she is a friend," Rachel said, "and she's not very big, so I guess— Oh, there's Janice and Marcie!" She wiped her face with a napkin Stella handed her. "Can I go play with them?"

"*May* I go play with them," Stella corrected gently.

"*May* I go?"

Stella wiped a corner of Rachel's mouth with a second napkin. "Yes, you may. Come back over here when it starts to get dark. And please don't run or you'll get sand in everybody's food."

"I won't." Rachel stood and walked over to where her friends stood waiting.

"Cyndi Lauper," Dodie murmured again, shaking her head.

"You're very good with Rachel," Judd told Stella after Rachel was out of earshot.

"Thank you." Stella gazed after Rachel. "As you see, she's made some friends already. Janice and Marcie are full of the devil, but they're basically nice kids." She hesitated. "They'd be in Rachel's class at school in the fall."

Judd met the pointed comment with silence. Rachel wouldn't be going to school here in the fall, and that was that, but he didn't want to get into it with Dodie listening.

Stella apparently felt no such compunction. She turned back to him, a desperate light in her eyes. "She reminds me so much of Michelle that I can't help dreaming, Judd. I checked out the school, and it's very good. I keep thinking that you could come here weekends. Every weekend, for that matter. You probably don't see much of Rachel during the week, anyway, and—"

"Stella." Allen put a hand on her arm. "Can't you see that Judd wants her, too?"

Stella's eyes were moist. "Yes, I can. Of course I can. I just . . . long for this child."

Dodie's attention seemed riveted on the scene. Judd could imagine the gossip this could provide at the hair salon. He cursed to himself.

"It seems to me," Allen said slowly, "that we all have to decide what's best for Rachel, disregarding our own needs."

Allen's calm rational statement hit Judd like a fist in the gut. He could deal with Stella's yearnings to replace her daughter, Michelle, with Rachel. It was a poignant situation, but Steve and Michelle had been clear that Judd was to raise their daughter. Still, they hadn't foreseen that Judd would remain a bachelor or that he'd be the head of a powerful company that sapped much of his time and energy.

He gazed across the crowded beach to where Rachel played down by the water with her two friends. She *did* seem very happy here. The mellow atmosphere that threatened to take the edge from his business sense might be exactly the right atmosphere for raising a child. Was he being selfish and unwise to insist she live with him in New York?

He felt uncomfortable with Dodie's apparent interest in him. Trying to ignore her avid stare, he glanced at Allen. "You're right. Rachel's well-being is the most important issue." His stomach clenched, but he forced himself to say the next sentence. "I promise you both I'll think very carefully about this."

Stella leaned over and kissed him on the cheek. "You're a good man, Judd." She glanced up at the soft violet sky. "And now one of us will have to go remind that object of our desires that it's getting dark and she has to stay with us now."

"I'll go get her." Judd stood.

Dodie started to rise. "I'll go, too."

Judd glanced down at her. "I think I'd better go alone," he said as gently as he could.

She stopped in midmotion and looked at him.

He held her gaze until he saw understanding there.

With a smile she rose and dusted off her leggings. "Can't blame a girl for trying," she said. "See you all later, okay?"

Judd sighed as she walked away.

"I'm sorry," Stella said. "I didn't know how to keep her from joining us without being rude. She was determined to make contact. She's had her eye on you ever since the concert this afternoon."

"But don't get a swelled head," Allen said. "Dodie goes after every eligible bachelor in town."

"Oh, Allen, it's not that bad. The poor woman hasn't been lucky with men, but she's still optimistically looking for her one true love. I like Dodie, but she's not your type, Judd."

"Whatever that is," Judd said with a smile. Yet even as he said it, he heard the sound of Kerry's voice rising on the evening breeze as she started a sing-along with the group gathering near the bonfire. He allowed himself one glance and was rewarded with the vision of her face and hair glowing in the firelight.

He forced himself to look away. "I'll get Rachel," he said.

The sand felt good between his toes as he made his way through the maze of blankets and beach towels toward Rachel. The French braid she'd been so proud of was coming loose as she and her two friends played chase with the gentle waves that lapped the shore. Her laughter pierced his heart. Had she laughed like that, so freely and with such delight, back in New York? He liked to think she had, but he wasn't sure.

He contrasted her friends here with the more sophisticated ones she had back home, the ones he'd hoped to separate her from by sending her away for the summer. Before long she'd be in high school, where she could get into real trouble if she chose the wrong kids to be with.

Maybe things would be different if he'd married and provided Rachel with a full-time female role model. He'd have to try harder on that score. Dodie Gibson wasn't the answer, but maybe there was someone out there.... Kerry's face flashed across his mind. No, not Kerry, or anyone like her. She wouldn't want a deal like that, anyway, not at this point in her life.

Still, if he could find the right woman to love, who would also love and guide Rachel, he might not have to consider this offer of Allen and Stella's. But time was running out. School enrollment wasn't that far away. Rachel was so important to him. So very important.

He cleared the lump from his throat and called her name.

She turned toward him, but something caught her eye and she turned back toward the water. "Look, Daddy!" She pointed a finger along the shoreline toward Eternity Harbor. Her voice shook with excitement. "They're coming!"

KERRY PUT DOWN her guitar and stood as the first sparkling lights appeared. The boat moved toward them along the shoreline, followed by another and another, each strung with hundreds of tiny bulbs. The charter-fishing-boat owners had outlined the cabins and the prows, while the sailboats were draped with lights that made a graceful arc from the top of the mast to the deck. As the parade of boats drew closer, the people gathered on the beach began to cheer, and as always, Kerry fought the urge to cry.

For the first eleven years of her life her father had been in the Fourth of July Parade of Lights with his fishing boat the *Leprechaun*. Fifteen years later, her brothers Sean, Dan and Ryan sailed a small sailboat, the *Leprechaun II*, in the same parade. The legacy the little boat represented created a lump in her throat.

She'd been so proud of her father, sailing his modest boat right along with the expensive pleasure yachts and the bigger, more elaborate trawlers. She remembered standing on this beach with her brothers and sisters and cheering until her throat hurt. Her mother would always caution her to protect her voice. For even then, her parents had dreamed of a glittering future for her. They'd scraped what they could out of a fisherman's income to give her voice and piano lessons.

The boats tooted their horns in salute as they came abreast of the gathering, and friends and family shouted greetings across the water. Kerry joined her family in waving and calling out to her brothers. Then she noticed Judd standing near the water's edge, his arm around his daughter. She wondered if he understood how much Rachel worshiped him. Kerry understood; she'd felt exactly the same way about her father.

Maybe that was why she'd said those things about Judd on the beach this morning. During Friday's piano lesson when Kerry had learned who Rachel's father was and that he was coming for the long weekend, Kerry had listened to Rachel lavish praise on her father, a father who wasn't going to be around except for three days all summer. Kerry had become angry that a man could be so blind to a little girl's love. After losing a wife, he of all people should understand that time was precious, that moments lost could never be replaced.

But who was she to judge someone she owed so much? He was willing to give her the chance she'd waited a lifetime for. If she succeeded, this might be the last Fourth of July she spent in Eternity for a long time. She watched the boats make a wide sweep and glide back toward the harbor. She stared hard, burning the memory into her mind.

A swishing sound from far down the beach ended in a reverberating boom, and over the water the first fireworks spilled red, white and blue stars against the night sky. A soft exclamation of wonder rose from the crowd.

As the embers drifted toward the water and were mirrored on its polished ebony surface, Kerry noticed that Judd and his daughter were walking back up the beach in her direction. Rachel broke away, apparently hurrying to reach her grandparents' blanket before the next shower of color appeared.

Judd's path would bring him right past where Kerry stood. Her heartbeat accelerated. She'd refrained from speaking to him all evening partly because Dodie Gibson seemed to have him in a hammerlock and partly because she was still confused about what had happened—or not happened—that afternoon.

Maybe he'd realized their reaction to each other was inappropriate. If so, she would follow his lead, but she still felt awkward being near him. It was dark now. Maybe he hadn't even seen her there. But as he approached, a splash of new fireworks illuminated his face, and she discovered he was looking directly at her.

What she saw in his eyes made her gasp. She'd expected the same guarded expression he'd adopted that afternoon, or perhaps friendly interest, or a comment about the festivities. Instead his gaze held such hot, desperate yearning it caused an answering tide of desire in her. She trembled, but could not look away from the heat of that fire. No one had ever looked at her that way. And she liked it. Then the sparkling fountain in the sky flickered out, and his face was thrown into shadow once more.

She couldn't speak, but he did. "See you in New York, Kerry," he said softly, and walked away.

5

Kerry stepped off the train in Penn Station, her garment-bag strap slung bandolier-style across her chest in one direction, her shoulder-bag strap across the other, to deter purse and suitcase snatchers. With a firm grasp on each strap, she mounted the stairs to the main terminal.

The crowd of people jostling her ran the gamut from smartly dressed mothers with toddlers to grimy-looking street people. A boy with one side of his head shaved and the remaining hair dyed purple walked shoulder to shoulder with a businessman who looked as if he'd stepped out of the pages of *GQ*. Despite their outward differences, everyone seemed to have the same sense of purpose and determination to get where they were going in a hurry.

But Kerry didn't want to be in such a hurry that she missed savoring this moment of triumph. She'd made it to the Big Apple. Someday she might be whisked in and out of the city by plane, maybe even private jet, but she would always remember when she first arrived on a commuter train from Eternity, when she first became part of this pulsing, whirling dervish of a city.

She arrived in the cavernous terminal and gazed around for the information booth. Judd's note had told her to go there, where someone would be waiting to take her to her hotel. The terminal held a bewildering number of shops selling newspapers, coffee, frozen yo-gurt, doughnuts, even haircuts and shoe shines.

"Coming through."

She jumped out of the way just as a burly man nearly wheeled a hand truck loaded with boxes over her foot. If she expected an apology, none came. Kerry smiled. Tough, these New Yorkers, like a twisted towel flicked across the backside, after the lullaby security of her hometown.

The brusque delivery man would probably get a belly laugh if he knew the contents of her large shoul-der bag. Her mother had warned her about the high food prices and insisted she take a few cans of tuna just in case Lighthouse Records didn't pick up the tab for all her meals. Then Grubby's wife had baked her a loaf of banana bread, which rested on top of the tuna so it wouldn't get hopelessly mashed. Rachel had contrib-uted chocolate bars for the train ride, and Hank had given her a handful of airplane-size liquor bottles to celebrate her first successful gig in New York. She'd taken the offerings more because she was touched than because she was worried that Lighthouse Records wouldn't provide.

At last she spied the information booth and headed toward it, mimicking the purposeful stride of the peo-ple streaming around her. She might as well start adapting to this pace of life. If she got her wish, New York would become her home.

She hadn't expected Judd to meet her—not really. Still, when a stocky, Mediterranean man held up a cardboard sign marked Muldoon, she deflated a little. She reminded herself that she wasn't here to see Judd, after all, despite the fact she'd spent a large part of the train ride thinking about that last burning look he'd given her on the beach in Eternity. Maybe she'd misread the look. She shook herself. She had a shot at a recording contract with one of the most up-and-coming labels in the business. What more did she want?

She approached the man with the sign. "I'm Kerry Muldoon. You must be from Lighthouse Records."

He nodded, his face showing no emotion.

"Which way to the car?"

"I'd better take that." He pointed to her garment bag.

Kerry wasn't used to having other people lug her stuff around, but she decided if she planned to be a star, she'd better get used to it.

The man waited with poorly disguised impatience while she divested herself of the garment bag and handed it to him. Then he led the way outside, where July heat settled over Kerry like a steam bath. She expected a taxi or a sedan, but instead, the man headed for a sleek gray limo sitting at the curb. Kerry gasped. Was Judd waiting inside the cool interior with a glass of champagne?

The man opened the passenger door for her. Heart thudding, she climbed in . . . and found the compartment empty. Another fantasy up in smoke. She'd have to get rid of these small-town romantic illusions. Still, she'd never ridden in a limo before. As the man got into the driver's seat, she smoothed the leather upholstery and wondered if she dared turn on the little television set. Too bad the guys in the band couldn't see her now, sitting in air-conditioned comfort, like Cleopatra on her barge, or Queen Elizabeth on her—

Her speculations ended as the car lurched forward and she was thrown back against the seat in a most unregal fashion. Scrambling upright to peer out the window at the traffic churning past, she gulped as the driver veered the long car around a swarm of yellow taxis and several lumbering buses. He drove with the concentration and urgency of a man propelling a hook and ladder to a five-alarm fire.

She'd planned to make conversation on the way to the hotel, but now she thought better of it. One distraction, one wrong move, and they'd both be road kill. After an especially close call, she gathered the courage to lean forward and speak through the small opening in the window separating the front seat from the back. "Is there some rush?"

"Nope. Got an hour before you have to be at Lighthouse. Hotel's about ten minutes away." He skirted a delivery truck and narrowly missed two pedestrians. "Plenty of time."

"Then could we slow down a little?"

The driver gunned the limo through a yellow light. "Gotta keep up with traffic."

"Oh." She supposed he had a point. Maybe driving slow through this chaos would only confuse people. Instead of hoping for a recording contract, maybe she ought to pray for surviving New York City traffic.

At last the limo screeched to a stop in front of the Salisbury Hotel on West Fifty-Seventh. A doorman helped Kerry out and guided her into a small but elegant lobby graced with chandeliers, burgundy leather armchairs and potted ferns.

She sighed with relief. This was more like it. Thank heavens she'd worn her suit for the trip. One needed a suit and modest heels, which she also wore, to feel adequate for this sort of understated good taste. But what on earth would she wear tomorrow? The clothes that had served her perfectly well in Eternity seemed unsophisticated and outdated now. She'd brought one cocktail dress, on loan from Emma Webster's shop. She could perform in that, at least, but her daytime wear was decidedly limited.

The limo driver brought in her garment bag, and even that trusty piece of luggage, which had seen her through her years as a student at Boston College, seemed shabby and worn against the richness of the lobby's carpet.

"I'll be outside in half an hour to take you to Lighthouse," the driver said, never cracking a smile. Then he left.

Kerry drew a deep breath and turned to the reservations clerk, who, bless him, did have a smile on his face. Kerry drank it in. "I'm Kerry Muldoon," she said for the second time within the past hour. That was another thing that seemed strange to her. Several months could pass in Eternity without the need to introduce herself. It seemed inconceivable that here was a whole city of people who didn't know who she was. *But they will*, she vowed. *They will.*

FORTY MINUTES LATER the taciturn limo driver deposited Kerry on Fifth Avenue. "Offices are on the eighteenth floor," he said, waving toward the revolving door of the slate gray building.

"Well . . . thanks." Kerry stepped forward with tip money in her hand, but the limo driver waved it away. "Been taken care of by Lighthouse," he said. What was almost a smile touched his lips. "Good luck."

"Thank you." She watched him pull away. That tiny smile had seemed reluctant, as if he couldn't really afford it or the wish of good luck. She wondered how many bright young hopefuls he'd dropped at this door, and how many had returned home, heartbroken. No wonder he hadn't made small talk or tried to find out anything about her. The less he got involved, the less he had to feel sorry for the hundreds who didn't make it. He couldn't know that she was the one in a thousand who would. Throwing back her shoulders, she marched through the revolving door.

Lighthouse Records had the entire eighteenth floor. The lobby, decorated in shades of blue, was dominated by a large oil painting of a lighthouse standing stark and white against a backdrop of angry clouds and tossing seas. Kerry paused in front of it, loving it instantly. It wasn't Eternity's lighthouse, but it almost could have been. She suddenly felt a little more at home.

"Kerry."

She turned to find Judd standing just inside the lobby door. But this wasn't the Judd who'd run the length of Eternity's beach, or walked barefoot to the water's edge to watch the Parade of Lights with his daughter. This man was the CEO of Lighthouse Records, from his dark blue double-breasted suit to his snowy white shirt and silk red-and-navy-striped tie. He looked taller, somehow, his shoulders broader, his eyes darker, more piercing.

"Hello, Judd." She stepped forward and held out her hand. She hoped he wouldn't notice it was shaking. "I made it."

"I had no doubt." His handshake was firm and lingered a moment as he looked into her eyes. "Are you ready?"

"Of course." She tried in vain to superimpose the other Judd—the one who'd vacationed with his daughter in Eternity—on to this Judd. The image wouldn't hold. This Judd had the crisp edge of the city about him, the scent of an expensive men's cologne. Only the slight hint of a lingering sunburn on his cheeks gave any indication of the person who'd sat on her stoop with his socks between his fingers.

He released her hand and turned toward another door leading off the lobby. "Then let's do it. I've set you up for a preliminary recording session, and then we'll talk about a couple of club gigs. You brought some sheet music?"

"In here." She patted her shoulder bag, which no longer contained tuna, candy, banana bread and tiny liquor bottles.

Judd glanced at the receptionist. "I'll be in Studio B if anyone needs me. Janet Jackson's manager was supposed to call this afternoon."

"Yes, Mr. Roarke. And don't forget about that benefit reception for the earthquake victims in Chile. Barbra Streisand's secretary called to remind you."

"Right." He turned to Kerry. "Would you like to go to the benefit? You wouldn't begin performing until tomorrow night, anyway."

Barbra Streisand? Kerry knew she'd have to get used to this and not have her heart stop beating every time she heard the casual mention of some music legend. For all she knew Barbra and Judd were next-door neighbors on Central Park West. "I'd love to go."

"Good." He started down a carpeted hallway lined with framed album covers. "The reception's at seven. We'll have a late dinner afterward and talk about your gigs."

She hurried to catch up with his long strides. She wanted to stop and examine the record jackets, visualize herself on the cover of a CD, but there seemed to be little time for contemplation in New York. Belatedly she realized he'd just included dinner with the evening plans. She would be Judd Roarke's date tonight, apparently. But she mustn't read too much into it. Correction. She mustn't read *anything* into it.

OUTWARDLY JUDD ROARKE behaved as he always did with new talent. He took Kerry into the control booth of Studio B and introduced her to Tom Ethridge, one of the best producers in the business, and Billy Wong, a senior engineer for Lighthouse. On a daily basis Billy turned mediocre into magic with his deft manipulation of the candy-colored buttons arranged in rows on the massive console. Judd looked forward to Billy's delight in Kerry's tone.

Then he took her out on the floor to meet the studio musicians, three guys who could make even an amateur sound good. With Kerry they should light up the studio.

She established a rapport with them immediately, which didn't surprise him. Soon he could tell he was extraneous, and he returned to the control booth. Sometimes he stayed to watch a first recording session, so he wasn't giving away much by hanging around.

But he had to be careful about touching her, or looking too long into those green eyes. He'd definitely assign someone else to take her around to the gigs. And he'd leave her alone after tonight, but the reception reminder had caught him by surprise, and he'd asked her before he'd had a chance to think. Then he'd compounded his lack of judgment by including dinner. Maybe they'd hook up with somebody else and he wouldn't end up alone with her. That would be best. He'd do that.

Tom punched the green Intercom button. "Signal when you're ready," he told Kerry. Then he turned the button off and swiveled his chair to face Judd. "Pretty girl. Where'd you say she was from?"

"Eternity, Massachusetts." Judd watched through the glass as Kerry put on headphones and adjusted the softball-size mike suspended from a boom.

"Isn't that the wedding place?"

"Yeah." He swallowed as she took off her suit jacket and tossed it over a stool. Her breasts lifted gently under her mint green blouse as she readjusted the headphones. The soft track lighting in the studio caressed her face as she glanced over the sheet music she'd arranged on the padded stand in front of her. He turned away before his interest became obvious to everyone in the booth.

"That could be a great angle, Judd," said Billy. "The girl from Eternity. You've probably thought of that."

Judd leaned his shoulder against a wall soundproofed with waffled foam padding. "She's a winner— looks, voice, stage presence, musical background."

Tom glanced at Kerry, who was sorting through the pages of her sheet music. "What's her specialty?"

"I don't see her falling into a niche so much as claiming the sort of broad pop-music audience Whitney Houston has."

Tom whistled. "Aiming for the big time, are we?"

"I think she can do it."

"Eternity's a small town," Billy said. "Does she have any concept how rough it is out there?"

Judd sighed. "Do any of them ever have a clue, Billy?"

"No, I guess not. They either toughen up as they go or they get out."

"Looks like she's ready," Tom said. He held up a hand to signal Kerry to begin. "Let's see what she's got," he said, and closed his hand into a fist.

Judd listened with his head down and forced himself to be analytical. She'd chosen an old Billy Joel tune, the rollicking "This Is My Life." Appropriate, he thought, this song of independence. His heart swelled at the strength in her voice. She was good. He glanced at Tom. For years he'd used Tom's reaction as a barometer for new talent. When Tom liked something, he wiggled his foot to the beat and quietly snapped his fingers. As Kerry sang, Tom's fingers and toes picked up her rhythm, and Judd smiled.

She finished the song and Tom switched on the intercom. "That sounded real good. Want to try it again, or do something else?"

"Something else." Her voice had a sweet ring to it that reminded Judd of tapping a piece of Waterford crystal gently with a fork.

"When you're ready, then," Tom said, and flipped off the intercom. When he turned toward Judd his nonchalance slipped a little. "Damn, Roarke, if I don't think you've found us a chart burner. Trust you to go on your one vacation of the year and come up with someone like this. Any more like her down in Eternity?"

Judd wasn't sure there were any more like Kerry in the world, let alone in Eternity. "Nope. We'll have to make do with her."

"It's days like this that make me glad I have stock in this crazy company. Have you run her past Erica?"

"I will when we get a good demo."

"Should be a piece of cake," Billy said.

Judd nodded. He was proud of the team he'd assembled. Nobody at Lighthouse believed in rubber-stamping a project. Erica Endicott, head of the artist-and-repertoire department, insisted on a demo created in the studio before she'd consider new talent. She swore by that method, saying it weeded out prima donnas who didn't have the patience for the meticulous studio work that had built the Lighthouse reputation.

Erica was nicely balanced by marketing director Henry Gridley, who demanded that new talent have a good live act. Technically Judd could override them both, but he never had. And he sure as hell wouldn't now with Kerry, not when he questioned his objectivity.

Tom held up his hand again as Kerry signaled to him. It occurred to Judd that he should leave and have Tom send Kerry down to his office when they had a tape they all liked. But he didn't want to leave. Tom made a fist and Kerry leaned close to the mike, eyes closed. Judd knew before she began that this would be a love song.

He might have guessed she'd choose one of his favorites, "I Will Always Love You." There'd been the Dolly Parton version and the Whitney Houston version. Now he had the Kerry Muldoon version, and it was a show stopper. He should walk out of this booth and start building his defenses. Because she was tearing them down with every note of this damn song. He'd asked her to sing for him. Now it seemed she was doing exactly that, singing for him and no one else in the world.

Of course it was all illusion. A good performer made each musical experience seem personal. He knew that too well to get taken in, swept away. Except this time his cynicism wasn't holding as Kerry's sweet words of love wrenched an answering emotion from deep in his gut.

She ended the song and opened her eyes. For one searing moment she looked up at him and he caught his breath. Then the drummer said something to her, and she glanced over her shoulder and laughed.

Snapped out of his fantasy, Judd turned from the window. The movement was abrupt enough for Tom to glance up, eyebrows raised.

"Work with her on those two and send her to my office when you're satisfied."

"Will do." Tom had a question in his eyes, but he didn't voice it, for which Judd was grateful.

Throughout the song Judd had been unaware of anything but Kerry and her seductive voice. For all he knew, Tom had been watching him, and if so, Tom knew more about Judd's emotions than he wanted to share.

"But for what it's worth, I think she's great," Tom ventured, looking straight at Judd.

"We'll see." He left the booth without looking back at Kerry.

6

KERRY SAW Judd's abrupt departure from the booth and panicked. He hadn't liked it. He regretted what was obviously a terrible mistake. In the cozy atmosphere of Eternity with a friendly audience she'd looked pretty good to him, but in the unforgiving confines of a recording booth all her flaws had stood out like beer cans on a beach. She clenched her hands and waited for the man named Tom to tell her she could go home now, and they'd be in touch. But of course they wouldn't be.

She pictured going back on the train and facing everyone in Eternity, especially Aunt June. Failure had never occurred to her until this moment. Now it seemed inevitable. Who did she think she was, anyway? New York was filled with great singers. Judd didn't need to scour the hinterlands for another artist for his label. She'd been damned lucky to get this far.

The intercom snapped on and she tensed.

"Kerry?" Tom said. "The boss wants us to polish those two tunes. Let's start with the Billy Joel number. I liked the intro, but let's punch in a new version of the second line. See if you can hit the pitch a tad cleaner."

"I . . . we're going to do it again?"

Ted laughed. "And again and again. You were great, almost perfect, but at Lighthouse almost isn't good enough. We're all anal retentives after perfection. And, Joe, pick up the tempo a little."

"Got it," the drummer said.

Kerry could only imagine they were being kind. She'd seen the way Judd had walked out of there, as if he could hardly wait to get away. She'd thought for a second, after the song was over and he'd looked at her, that she'd had a strong effect on him. He'd looked . . . transfixed. Maybe what she'd interpreted as fascination had been horror, instead.

"And the keyboard might be a little heavy in the opening chords, Woody," Tom continued. "Tone it down a little. Not much, just a little."

"Sure."

Kerry tried to concentrate, tried to follow directions, but she couldn't put the picture of Judd striding from the booth out of her mind. She loused up her phrasing on the next line of the song. Then she came in a beat too soon. Tom coached her patiently, and the third try at the line was free of any noticeable mistakes.

Kerry had recorded demos before. She knew it was tedious work as a song was pieced together phrase by phrase. Given Judd's reaction, she couldn't understand why everyone was bothering to spend the time, but she slogged along because she didn't have the courage to question Tom about the futility of the project.

Finally they must have decided to stop torturing her.

"That's good enough for now," Tom said over the intercom. "Judd wanted to see you in his office when we were done."

Here it comes, Kerry thought, putting on her jacket and gathering up her music. She shook hands with the musicians and the men in the control booth before taking the long walk back down the hall to the lobby. A lead weight formed in her stomach as she thought of the high hopes she'd had a couple of hours ago. She had no interest in the framed album covers on the wall now. She wouldn't be joining the gallery, so what difference did it make who else was up there?

In the lobby she got directions to Judd's office and took another short hallway, which ended in a set of double doors. They were hand carved and featured a bas-relief of a lighthouse on each door. Lighthouses were fast becoming her least favorite symbol. She wondered if she'd be able to look at the one in Eternity without bursting into tears.

She rapped on the heavy doors and heard Judd's brisk "Come in" as a death knell to all her dreams, not to mention the dreams of an entire town that believed she would be a star. She opened the door.

When she'd first arrived at the Lighthouse offices he'd come out to the lobby to meet her. Now he'd barricaded himself behind his massive desk. Her gaze flicked over framed industry awards, autographed pictures of well-known performers, and a shelf full of Grammys. The tall windows facing Fifth Avenue looked out on the glitter and whipping flags of Rockefeller Center. The room was all about success. Kerry didn't belong here.

Judd had taken off his suit coat and loosened his tie. His hair looked rumpled, as if he'd been running his fingers through it a lot in the past two hours. He'd probably been debating how to tell her to hit the road.

As she'd expected, his expression was distant as he tossed down his pen and leaned back in his swivel chair. "Have a seat," he said, gesturing toward one of the dark blue leather chairs positioned in front of the desk.

"That's okay." She didn't want to be any closer to him than necessary so she could beat a hasty retreat when he delivered the bad news. In fact, she'd help him deliver it. "Look, it was great of you to bring me down here and give me a chance, but I realize now that the odds are much higher than I imagined."

He leaned forward, his impassive mask gone. "Is that right?"

"Eternity, Massachusetts, may think I'm a big deal, but that doesn't make it so, does it?"

He stared at her, a frown creasing his forehead.

"And don't think you still have to take me to the reception tonight, but if you don't mind, I'd like to stay at the hotel, instead of going home this afternoon. I'm sure you'll be charged for the room, anyway, and it'd be easier for me to catch a train in the morning, when—"

He stood and braced both fists on the desk. "What in God's name are you talking about?"

"Going home."

"You've been in New York three hours and you're ready to go home?"

Now it was her turn to stare. Why hadn't he picked up his cue? She'd handed him the perfect chance to let her down easy.

He rounded the desk and came toward her, his expression thunderous. "I can't believe you don't have more spunk than that. Not after the scene I witnessed on the beach. I can't believe that just because Tom asked you to polish those numbers you've decided you can't take the pressure."

"I—"

"But if that's the way you feel, you're better off going home. Because the pressure gets a whole lot worse before you hit the top, babe."

"But..." She choked in confusion and had to try again. "But you don't think I'll make it to the top!"

"What gave you that imbecilic idea?"

"You walked out of the recording session! No, I take that back. You *stalked* out of the recording session."

Slowly his features softened. He reached out as if to touch her, then dropped his hand back to his side. "You misunderstood," he said softly.

"You didn't hate it?"

"No."

"But I thought. . . ."

"I can see what you thought." His eyes were golden again, as they had been on that day he'd sat on her front stoop. "I'm sorry. I had . . . some business waiting and I had to leave. I should have said something to you before I left."

She took a deep breath. *She wasn't going home.* But she felt like a fool. Of course this busy executive couldn't hang around a recording studio all afternoon offering praise. She flushed. "I'm the one who should apologize. You have dozens of artists, a huge business to run and more responsibility than I can probably imagine. It's perfectly logical that you left the control booth without explaining yourself. You shouldn't ever need to."

"That's not true. We don't operate like that at Lighthouse. We treat each other with respect. Nobody's allowed to be pompous, especially me."

"Nevertheless, I have to learn to be less sensitive."

He sighed and glanced away. "I suppose you do." His telephone buzzed and he turned toward his desk. "Excuse me." He reached across the desk to pick up the receiver and propped one hip on the polished edge of the desk while he talked. Kerry thought he looked almost as sexy as he did in his jogging shorts. "Yes . . . okay. I'll be with them in a minute. Thanks, Lois." He hung up the phone and turned back to her.

"You see?" She smiled and gestured toward the phone. "A busy man."

"Oh, yeah." He grinned back at her. "Without me the world wouldn't turn."

When he smiled like that he certainly made her world turn, Kerry thought. Okay, so she had a crush on the boss. She'd read somewhere that fantasies only become a problem when you act on them. No one had to know what was in her heart when she looked at Judd Roarke. "Is there anything else you needed from me or should I head back to my hotel?"

His eyes darkened momentarily. "I guess there's nothing. If you'll wait a minute, Lois can call Zorba."

"The chauffeur?"

"Yeah."

Kerry laughed. She was beginning to like New York again. "That's his name, really?"

"No, but he gets a kick out of calling himself that. He's Greek and an old Anthony Quinn fan. Anyway, he can take you back, but Lois will have to call him, see if he's free. You can ask her on the way out."

"Never mind." Now that she knew he wasn't giving her the boot, Kerry felt as if she could do anything. "I'll catch a cab. I might as well get used to doing that."

"You don't have to—"

"I think I do. I want to prove I can be a New Yorker."

"If you say so. I'll pick you up at the Salisbury about six forty-five, assuming you still want to go."

"Of course." She almost skipped as she left his office. He hadn't hated her recording session. She was still here.

And tonight she'd be with Judd all evening.

JUDD TRIED to focus on his call, which was the much-awaited one from Janet Jackson's manager. Handled right, the manager might convince Janet to give Lighthouse a try. Judd knew he wasn't handling it right, and finally he asked the manager if they could discuss the matter later.

The manager sounded startled but agreed. Judd hung up and leaned back in his chair, eyes closed. He'd hurt Kerry. Already. He'd been so wrapped up in his own reactions he hadn't thought how his behavior would look to her.

A rap sounded on the door. Judd opened his eyes just as Tom stuck his head in.

"You busy, Judd?"

"No, come on in. How'd the session go after I left?" He figured he knew the answer.

"Not great." Tom walked over and balanced on the edge of a blue leather chair, his hands dangling between his knees. "There was magic in those tunes the first time she sang them, but after you left she lost the spark. Don't get me wrong. She worked hard. She's not one of those spoiled bitches Erica worries about. But she struggled. She's new, though. She'll probably smooth out."

Judd felt Tom watching him. He purposely made his expression bland. "Sure she will. Probably got the jitters."

"I guess that's possible, although she didn't act nervous while you were there. I'd have thought it'd be the other way around, that she'd be less nervous when you left the booth."

Judd dropped his gaze. "Yeah, well, I screwed up, Tom. She told me a little while ago that when I left so quickly she thought I hated what I'd heard."

Tom nodded slowly. "It was a pretty fast exit."

"Pretty stupid, too. I've apologized to her, so I think tomorrow will be better. We'll run through some complete sets, get her ready for her club gigs."

"Sounds good." Tom continued to gaze at him.

Judd couldn't ignore it any longer. "Okay, Tom, what's on your mind?"

"Are you even aware that she has a huge crush on you?"

A wave of heat washed over him. "You have an overactive imagination, Tom. Always have. That's why you're so damned creative."

"Ignore me if you want, but she was on fire with those first two numbers, and I think she was singing them just for you."

Judd didn't want to hear that. "Good technique, that's all. And then she thought I didn't like it, and I'm the head honcho, so she freaked out. Perfectly natural."

"Yeah, that could be one explanation." Tom slapped his palms on his knees and stood. "I guess we'll find out tomorrow, huh? That is, if you don't sit in."

"I have meetings all day tomorrow." And he'd keep on having meetings, Judd decided as Tom left the office. Gridley from marketing could take her to her gigs, and he'd stay completely in the background. If she had a crush on him he didn't want to know. He was having enough trouble dealing with his own libido, without factoring in hers.

KERRY OPENED a can of tuna with her Swiss army knife and ate it with a plastic fork before she put on her cocktail dress. Undoubtedly there would be food at the reception, but with her luck she'd be so nervous she'd spill something on John Mellencamp or whatever luminary would be there, so she didn't plan to eat. Judd had mentioned a late dinner, but Kerry was used to eating at a normal time, and she was starving. This sort of schedule would take some getting used to. In the meantime she blessed her mother for insisting on the cans of tuna. Nobody would know her secret except the maid, she thought, dropping the empty can delicately in the trash.

She washed her hands and brushed her teeth before she took the cocktail dress out of its plastic bag. Made of red satin, strictly dry-cleanable, it had to last the length of her stay.

When she'd tried it on in the back room of Emma Webster's shop, she'd felt like a star. A slit up one side to midthigh revealed a tantalizing bit of leg without being gauche. The bodice hugged her curves and dipped just enough in front and back to be sensual, not tacky. Red satin pumps and a necklace and earrings of Austrian crystal were also on loan from Emma's shop. When Emma had dressed her, with her mother and Aunt June looking on, Kerry had felt like Cinderella being prepared for the ball. She still felt that way tonight. Her hair, swept up on top of her head, contributed to the illusion.

She turned once in front of the mirror. Maybe her coach would change into a pumpkin at midnight, but until then she'd enjoy an evening with the prince.

The phone rang and her heartbeat quickened. She held the receiver to her ear and swallowed.

"I'm in the lobby," Judd said.

"I'll be right down." Perhaps she shouldn't sound so eager, she thought as she replaced the receiver and reached for the beaded evening bag Emma had included with the package. A true New Yorker might have requested a few more minutes. But Kerry couldn't stay in her hotel room another second, knowing Judd was downstairs waiting for her. Let him think what he wanted.

She stepped off the elevator and paused to take in the splendor of Judd in a midnight dark tux and pleated white shirt. He truly looked like a prince tonight.

He stepped forward, his gaze intense. "The lady in red," he murmured, offering her his arm. "There doesn't seem to be a color you can't wear."

She linked her bare arm through his jacketed one and her fingers closed over the muscles of his forearm. A current of awareness zinged through her, making her vibrate like a tuning fork. "I look pretty awful in orange."

"You'd have to prove it to me." He led her past the uniformed doorman, who tipped his hat and smiled.

Kerry smiled back. She'd never felt this high. Ahead of them Zorba waited, also in uniform for the occasion, his hand on the open door of the gray limo. "Hello, Zorba," she said, flashing another smile.

"Hello, Miss Muldoon." His expression was grave, but there was a twinkle in his eyes. Did he believe now that she wasn't just another hopeful soon to be discarded?

Judd handed her into the cool interior, where the tinted windows filtered out the daylight that remained on this warm summer night. She slid across the seat and he slipped in next to her. An open bottle of champagne sat in an ice bucket on the console in front of them. Kerry glanced to the front of the limo. If Zorba drove the way he had that afternoon, they'd both be covered in champagne inside of five seconds.

To her surprise Zorba allowed the limo to idle at the curb while Judd poured two flutes of the bubbly liquid.

He handed one to her. "Accept this as my apology for throwing you a curve today."

She gazed at him, dazzled beyond words.

"Here's to a rewarding career," he said, touching the rim of his glass to hers.

"Thank you." The words came out a whisper. She raised the glass to her lips and drank as Zorba eased the limo into traffic like a dolphin gliding seamlessly into an ocean wave. None of this seemed real to Kerry, who expected any minute to wake up in the four-poster antique bed in her rented colonial.

"I also have to apologize for starving you to death," Judd said. "I should have told you to order from room service if you got hungry."

Kerry glanced at him, so magnificent in his tux, so elegant and sophisticated. In her overwhelmed state, she blurted out the story about the tuna. To her relief he laughed.

"A Swiss army knife?" he asked, grinning at her. "Are you packing it in that little bag right now?"

"Goodness, no."

"Too bad. You never can tell what we'll encounter between here and the Village. By the way, how did you make out with the taxi this afternoon?"

"It took me six tries, but I finally found someone smaller than me I could shove out of the way so I could nab one."

Judd laughed again. "I think you're turning into a New Yorker, at that." He leaned back and crossed his ankle over his knee. "I've never met a woman who carries a Swiss army knife," he said, glancing at her over the rim of his champagne flute. "Any more surprises I should know about?"

Kerry liked him best when he relaxed. He was pretty virile and exciting as the take-charge CEO of Lighthouse Records, but when he dropped the air of authority a little, he made her heart turn over. "Well, one of my ancestors on my mother's side was hanged as a witch," she said.

"No kidding? In Salem?"

"No. Connecticut. The poor woman wouldn't confess, so they strung her up."

"And was she a witch, do you think?"

Kerry gazed at him. "Depends on whether you believe in witches."

7

AT THAT MOMENT Judd believed completely in witches. Green-eyed ones in heart-stopping red dresses who made him forget every resolution he'd made to stay clear of Kerry Muldoon.

Selfishly, he no longer wanted to go to the reception. An intimate little jazz club in the Village held far more appeal—the wail of a sax, candlelight, a bottle of wine and afterward, those tempting lips against his, the slide of satin under his fingers. . . .

"I don't know about witches," he said, "but I believe in spells."

She held his gaze, her glass halfway to her lips. "Aye, and the wee people?" she asked in that enchanting brogue he'd heard her use before. He knew she'd lived in Massachusetts all her life, knew the brogue was more playful than authentic, but it charmed him, anyway.

"Sometimes."

She gave him a sly look. "Sure 'and I would've taken you for a more practical man."

"I was a musician before I was a businessman, and you know what they say about musicians."

Her emerald eyes gleamed. "You were a wild and crazy lad when you were younger, then?"

He thought of the gigs until two in the morning, the after-hours jam sessions that lasted till dawn. He hadn't touched his sax for years, but he could still taste the bamboo reed flavored with scotch, smell the smoke in the clubs, an equal mix of tobacco and pot. And he could still see Suzanne crooning into the mike, her smoky voice bringing the band whatever acclaim it had ever had. He'd loved her more than the music, but she'd loved the music more than him. She'd considered him a hindrance to her career, so she'd dumped him. She might have made it big, if the drugs that had apparently replaced their passion hadn't killed her.

"I'm sorry." Kerry touched his sleeve, her Irish accent abandoned. "I didn't mean to pry."

He gazed at her. "Tom asked me today if you knew how rough it is out there."

"I can guess."

"You'd never guess, Kerry. It's a catch-22. You have to have the drive and ambition to make it, but that kind of single-mindedness will change you. Some things are lost along the way. Sometimes very important things."

"Yet every day you encourage people along that path."

"Maybe I like making money."

She shook her head. "I don't believe it's only about money."

"No." He sipped his champagne. "We need music. Inspired or sentimental, funny or crazy. It taps into our subconscious, brings out what gets buried under the garbage."

"I couldn't live without music."

He glanced at her. "Neither could I. But the people who give it to us are sometimes consumed by the gift." He swallowed the last of his champagne. "Well that's enough amateur philosophy for one night. We're almost there. Tonight will begin the word-of-mouth campaign that an exciting new talent's in town. I've booked you for the next three nights at Compulsions, and over the weekend at the Besotted Fox. Try to drop that into the conversation whenever you can."

"Okay." Her eyes were wide, her breathing shallow.

"Does the idea of performing in a New York club scare you?"

"It petrifies me."

"You, the lady with the Swiss army knife?"

Her answering smile was weak. "I suppose I could threaten to slash the audience to ribbons if they didn't clap loud enough."

Instinctively, he covered her hand with his. "You'll be fine." Her soft hand trembled under his. His grip tightened and he fought the urge to lean over and taste those softly parted lips.

"Will you be there?"

Warnings sounded in his head and he released her hand. "No, I...have some things to do tomorrow night."

"Of course. There I go again. Sorry." She looked away and sipped her champagne.

He felt like the worst kind of heel. She needed his support, and he was denying it. But he had to. Even now, her perfume swirled through his senses and it took all his restraint not to crush her to him. "Tomorrow I'll introduce you to Henry Gridley, director of our marketing department." *And he's also single,* Judd suddenly remembered with dread. "He'll go with you. We wouldn't toss you out there alone."

"I must seem like a baby," she said, still not looking at him.

Not even close, he thought, following the smooth line of her throat down to the graceful curve of crystals encircling her neck. "Most people would be nervous jumping into the club scene, but I'm afraid it's necessary. My people always feel better if they can see new talent in a club setting."

"People? You mean others from Lighthouse will be there besides Mr. Gridley?"

"You'll never know it. They'll just slip in and out."

She took a deep breath. "No pressure, right?"

"Hey, once you get over being nervous, you'll be fine, no matter who's watching. You're a born performer, Kerry. We both know that."

She turned back to him, her expression open and trusting. Her voice was soft. "But will I be consumed by the gift, Judd?"

IF THERE WAS a special spot in heaven for musicians, this loft in Greenwich Village would do nicely as a prototype, Kerry thought. She became giddy from being in the same room with so many stars she'd admired. Other than a few artfully hung cascades of white silk and strategic lighting, the loft was bare, allowing the space to be decorated with people, instead of objects. Within ten minutes Kerry met Bruce Springsteen, who seemed to be very good friends with Judd, Michael Bolton and Linda Ronstadt.

Once in a while a camera flashed, but the photographers were unobtrusive. Kerry suspected they'd been carefully chosen so that the event would get some publicity but not turn into a feeding frenzy for the media.

A combo played in one corner, and every once in a while a guest would wander over and take a turn with one of the instruments or sing one of his or her old standards to enthusiastic applause from their peers. Food was exotic and plentiful, but Kerry stuck to her vow of not eating, on the chance she'd ruin her precious red dress. She sipped mineral water, instead of wine, not wanting anything to cloud her memory of tonight. She tried to turn herself into a human video camera to capture it all for the benefit of everyone back in Eternity.

Somewhere along the way she lost Judd in the crowd, but people were so nice to her she didn't feel deserted in the least. Many were curious about Eternity, and several said they'd plan their next marriage in the chapel, to improve their usually dismal odds for marital success. Kerry began to understand what her stardom could mean for the town. Several merchants had banded together to form Weddings, Inc., a complete wedding planning service. A few famous entertainers using the service would ensure its success.

Kerry was congratulating herself on how well she was handling the pressures of hobnobbing with the stars when Judd put a hand on her shoulder. "Several people have asked if you'd sing."

Kerry spilled half her glass of mineral water down his shirt. "Now?"

He took out a handkerchief and mopped at his shirt. "I take it you're not crazy about the proposal."

Kerry's heartbeat thundered in her ears. "But Judd, *everybody's* here."

He tucked the handkerchief into his jacket pocket. "That's the idea." His golden gaze challenged her. "What are you made of, Muldoon? Are you the pot of gold at the end of the rainbow or are you the Blarney stone?"

"Don't throw that Irish malarkey at me at a time like this. I need that handkerchief."

He retrieved it and handed it to her.

She dabbed at her damp temples and wiped her sweating palms. "You mean right now?"

"I figured you'd do 'New York, New York.' I know you don't need music for it. If you want I'll get a few people to imitate sea gulls."

"You are not funny."

"That's too bad, because if you'd laugh, you'd release that tension in your diaphragm and you just might be able to pull this off."

She gazed into his eyes.

"It's the chance of a lifetime, Kerry. I have people under contract at Lighthouse who would give their firstborn to perform in front of this group."

She started to hyperventilate. "I . . . just didn't . . . expect . . ."

"Great. Now you're turning blue." He took her glass. "Cup your hands and blow into them."

She followed his advice and the room stopped spinning.

"Shall I tell the band you'll do that number?"

She swallowed.

"Pretend they're a bunch of well-dressed sea gulls. You can even take your shoes off if that would help. I'd truck in a load of sand, but I think people would get tired of waiting for your number."

She took a long, shaky breath. "I'll do it."

"Good. Now don't pass out on me while I tell the band. What key?"

She told him and he walked away. Her head buzzed, but she kept taking deep breaths and thinking of how much this would mean to her town. Everyone there had been so good to her. She must not fail them now. She walked to the small raised platform where the combo had been performing all evening. The man playing the bass fiddle smiled at her. She smiled back, although the effort made her feel as if her skin would crack.

A flock of sea gulls. That's what she would pretend the audience was, as Judd had suggested. The band played the introduction and she took the mike out of its stand. A flock of sea gulls. Except for Judd. She needed to see his face. She scanned the gathering, blotting out recognition of anyone else. Finally she found him over to her left, his smile soft. He nodded gently. A small stream of confidence flowed into her, and she began.

At first she sang without moving, but as the music filled her, years of training took over and she began to deliver the song as she'd practiced so many times on the beach. The slit up one side of her dress allowed her enough freedom to swing her hips and stride back and forth across the small platform.

The audience began to sway in time with her, and then to clap in rhythm. She had them. She had them! The smile she flashed at Judd felt like it had enough wattage to light up Radio City Music Hall. As she approached the climactic ending of the song, she made a decision. Once again she changed the words and flung herself into the final phrase with a rousing, "It's up to you, Judd Roarke, Judd Roarke!"

The hoots of laughter and enthusiastic applause splashed over her like a shower of glittering confetti, and she joined in the laughter out of sheer joy. She'd done it. New York was her town!

She glanced at Judd, saw the expression in his eyes. No, she wasn't wrong about that look. Maybe, just maybe, Judd would be hers, too.

IF KERRY HAD IMAGINED her late dinner with Judd would be an intimate affair, she'd obviously misjudged. He'd invited three executives from other recording companies and their wives to join them at a boisterous basement restaurant with loud music and a rowdy crew of waiters wearing Rollerblades. Judd sat at the far end of the table from her, as if deliberately putting distance between them.

"I think Judd invited us so he could gloat," said one rotund man with glasses.

Kerry had forgotten what company he represented. Her head was spinning from the number of people she'd met that night, and the warm glow of her triumph had faded as exhaustion took over. She wondered why Judd had invited all these people. Surely he didn't want to give some other studio a chance at her, yet all three executives pressed business cards into her hand and predicted how much better her career would progress if she left Lighthouse and signed with them.

She finally decided, as the long meal ended, that Judd was testing her loyalty. And perhaps her endurance, too. She'd been up since five that morning, and a glance at her watch confirmed it was after one now. Adrenaline had taken her this far, but it wouldn't carry her much longer.

"I think I'd better get Kerry back to her hotel," Judd said, glancing down the table at her. "She looks whipped."

"It's been quite a day." She managed a smile.

Judd tucked several bills into the leather-bound folder containing the tab. "This one's on me. I figure the winner pays, right?"

"See?" the rotund man pointed out. "He *is* gloating!"

"I think the rest of us should take a trip to Eternity," said a tall thin man with a mustache. "Like fools we've been expecting the talent to come to us, when actually it's hiding out in little fishing villages in Massachusetts."

Kerry managed another smile as Judd helped her out of her chair. "You've all been great. I couldn't have asked for a warmer welcome to New York."

They all chorused their goodbyes as Judd guided her past the whizzing waiters. He stopped at the reservation desk and asked the maître d' to call a cab before taking Kerry's elbow and escorting her up a flight of stairs to the street. "When it's this late, I usually don't call Zorba," he explained. "I hope you don't mind."

"Of course not." But it occurred to her that her chariot had indeed turned into a yellow pumpkin and the prince didn't seem the slightest bit interested in glass slippers. Maybe he only saw her as a commodity, after all. His intense gazes might only mean he was thinking about the profits she could make for his company. At any rate, she was too tired to dwell on the matter.

Even at this hour vehicles still zipped down the street, horns honking. The pace never seemed to stop.

"We'll be sending musicians with you tomorrow night," Judd said, standing with his hands in his pockets. "If you want any backup singers, say so. Personally, I wouldn't—"

"I'm not used to backup."

"Good."

She noticed someone huddled in a doorway. She couldn't tell whether it was a man or a woman, but obviously the person had nowhere to go. At least the night was warm. Kerry wondered if she'd be one of the people passing out blankets to the homeless this winter. One thing was for sure, she wouldn't be able to ignore them.

A cab swerved to the curb and Judd helped her inside. "You don't have to come with me," she said as he stepped in after her.

"I think I do."

She was too tired to argue with him. Probably he didn't want to leave his precious commodity out alone at this hour. It was a very different feeling, being valued for her earning potential, instead of herself. She leaned her head against the seat and closed her eyes as Judd gave the cab driver the name of the hotel. When the cab veered back into traffic, she drifted into a doze.

In her dream she was still riding in the cab, but Judd's behavior had changed. He cradled her in his arm and stroked her hair, not because she'd one day become a big star for Lighthouse Records, but because he cherished her. She put her arms around his neck and snuggled close, inhaling the woodsy scent of his after-shave. Even in the dream she knew this wasn't appropriate behavior toward the CEO of the company she hoped would put her under contract, but he felt so good she couldn't pull away.

"Kerry."

She reluctantly fought her way out of sleep and opened her eyes. Two facts immediately hit her consciousness. The cab was no longer moving. And she *was* inside the circle of Judd's arm, her head on his shoulder. His eyes were shadowed, and he was looking down at her, his mouth close to hers.

She held perfectly still, caught in the warmth of her dream—if it had been a dream.

"Witch," he whispered, and lowered his head.

Warm and sweet, so sweet. She moaned softly at the richness of his mouth, like dark chocolate dipped in brandy. And the promise of those lips ... A world of delights shimmered in the distance, conjured up from the sensuous pressure of his mouth.

Slowly he straightened, his gaze meshed with hers. "It's late," he said, his voice thick.

What now? Should she invite him to come in with her? Or were his words a dismissal?

He touched her cheek. "You need your sleep. Zorba will pick you up at eight."

A dismissal, then. Apparently he could kiss her and send her away. Was this the way men behaved in the big city? Like a person drugged, she put distance between them. He stepped out of the cab and offered his hand. She looked up at him as she climbed out.

"You were wonderful tonight," he said.

Anger pierced her sensual daze, and she was tired enough not to care what she said to him. She removed her hand from his. "Referring to what, exactly? My performance at the party, my loyalty to you when other executives tried to woo me away, or my kiss? I know I'm just a small-town girl, but I haven't a clue how to react to you."

He uttered a soft oath and turned away.

"I suppose I'm showing my lack of sophistication. I suppose you kiss all the women who record for you."

He turned back to her, his gaze troubled. "No, I don't."

"Oh. So it was a momentary lapse and now you regret it."

"It was a momentary lapse. I don't regret it."

"Oh, really?" She stepped toward him, frustration making her bold. "Want to try it again?"

He kept his hands at his sides, his tone mild. "More than you know."

"But?"

"It wouldn't be a good idea. For either of us."

"Speak for yourself," she said, and whirled past the doorman.

8

A CONTROL HE DIDN'T KNOW he possessed kept him from going after her. He stood there, not giving a damn that the cab's meter was running and the doorman was staring at him as if he'd lost his mind. Which he almost had.

Finally, when he was confident his step would take him toward the cab and not through the door of the Salisbury, he moved. His need for Kerry was getting out of hand. He'd better find a way to drain off some of that heat she was generating in him. And there was a way.

Getting back into the cab, he gave the driver an address on Central Park West, not far from his own apartment. Even on a week night, the woman he wanted to see had never turned him away. But when the cab stopped at the elegant apartment house Judd remained seated, listening to the meter tick.

"This is the place, mister."

Judd decided he must indeed be crazy. Inside this building was a remedy for satisfying his physical needs, and yet he couldn't go in. This woman, a business executive with no time or inclination for a romantic relationship, had been his answer for quite a while. With Rachel around he hadn't wanted complicated entanglements with the few women he'd dated.

But tonight it felt wrong to go through that door.

"The meter's still tickin', so it don't matter to me if we sit here all night," the cabbie said.

Judd opened the door and stepped out. He paid the cabbie and turned toward the building entrance. Then with a muttered oath he turned away. Taking off his tux jacket and slinging it over his shoulder, he started down the block toward his own apartment.

The dense foliage of Central Park hung motionless and still, but a percussion section of insects added a Latin rhythm to the hum of passing cars. Judd's hearing had always been acute, but tonight all his senses seemed fine-tuned. He smelled the smoke from someone's cigarette, a lingering perfume from an open car window, the acrid scent of warm asphalt. The fabric of his clothes caressed his body as he moved.

Ah, Kerry.

Funny, probably some of the people at the party tonight assumed he was sleeping with her. Those who knew him well wouldn't assume that, because the word was out among his close friends that Judd Roarke's first priority was his daughter. They knew he'd never parade women through the apartment he shared with Rachel, or fail to come home at night, or allow himself to be the subject of rumors she'd hear. If he needed a sexual outlet, he handled that need with discretion.

Except that tonight the old formula hadn't applied. When he'd held Kerry as she slept on the cab ride home, an emotion more complicated than desire had circled him in its net. For some imbecilic reason, he felt compelled to be true to a woman he dared not have.

KERRY WORKED so hard the following day she had little time to think. From the moment she walked into the studio at eight-fifteen until Henry Gridley told her it was time to go home and change for the gig, she didn't see daylight. Sandwiches were brought in for lunch and for the dinner they wolfed down before preparing for the evening's performance.

"Do any of you have families?" she asked the three men who would make up the band at Compulsions that night.

"Sure," said Woody, the keyboardist, around a bite of liverwurst. "I have a wife and kid, Joe has a wife and two kids. Paul's engaged."

"How do you manage? Or rather, how do they manage?"

Joe laughed. "Everybody bitches a lot, but this is what I do, and I love it. When I get into this studio, time stops for me. Nothing else is important. We shut out the world and do our music."

"And sometimes people get divorced over it," Woody said. "I didn't mention that this is my second wife."

"But if it's in your blood," Paul said, "you can't help yourself, right, Kerry?"

"You're right," Kerry said. "I've wanted this ever since I was a little kid."

Paul included them all with a wave of his ham on rye. "Same for us. We're hard-core. Can't be rehabilitated."

Kerry grinned at them, recognizing kindred spirits. It was the same bond she'd shared with the Honeymooners back in Eternity. She'd decided to give Grubby a call after her last set tonight. She might get him out of bed, but telling him about last night's party—and all the celebrities who were there—would be worth it. Grubby would be impressed that some of the celebrities might even try and catch her show tonight.

But Judd wouldn't. She hadn't seen him all day. Last night's kiss was starting to seem like a dream.

With a sigh she wrapped the last of her turkey sandwich and stuffed it back in the paper bag from the deli. She wasn't very hungry, anyway.

THAT NIGHT when Henry Gridley called from the lobby of the Salisbury, Kerry contrasted her nervous energy with the breathless excitement she'd felt the night before when Judd had been waiting for her. Tonight was just as important to her career as the night before had been, but the bubbling magic she'd felt then was gone. Judd seemed to have taken it with him.

Henry was short and blond with the body of a dockworker and the mind of a circus barker. As marketing director he'd already suggested to Kerry how he'd package her for the road. Kerry had an image of butcher paper and strapping tape. And when she was packaged—with a new hairstyle, sexier clothes, more elaborate makeup—would she still be Kerry Muldoon?

"Sensational," Henry said when he glimpsed her coming toward him in her red dress. "Maybe red will become your signature color."

"If I make it," she said with a smile. "I haven't even signed a contract yet."

"You will." Henry ushered her out the door. "Judd seldom guesses wrong. He played your demo during a staff meeting today, and Erica from A and R liked what she heard. If I testify that you have a good live act, then you're pretty much in."

"Then I'd better do well tonight." Kerry said hello to Zorba and got into the limo. Amazing how the interior climate of the limo had shifted from sensuous to humdrum, she thought as she glanced at Henry.

"I read the bio you filled out today," he said. "Impressive musical training. You've obviously been preparing for this all your life. Must have been expensive."

"It was." Kerry thought of the sacrifices her family had made when she was young, and how Aunt June had picked up the burden of her lesson expenses after her father died. "I was lucky to have some help along the way. Thank goodness I qualified for college scholarships, too."

"And you were never lured by the idea of a husband and kids?" His gaze held an interest she could easily interpret. That, coupled with his ringless left hand, told her he was assessing her availability.

She laughed. "Get married and waste all that money and effort? Not on your life."

"That's still the difficult choice we give women, I guess. It's a shame so many guys can't accept having a wife who wants a high-powered career."

She appreciated his politically correct comments, even if she suspected he was advancing his own cause. She might as well put a halt to his fishing expedition, though. Henry wasn't her type. She shrugged. "I think romantic entanglements of any kind at this stage in my career would only be a distraction."

"Probably right." He settled back in his seat, obviously taking the hint. "Marketing has been tossing around ways to promote you. We'd take the small-town angle, I think, maybe work in the Irish ancestry. When did the Muldoons first come to this country?"

"My great-great-great-grandfather Sam, who was a wonderful singer, by the way, settled in Eternity before the Civil War. My mother's family was English. Their line dates all the way back to the sixteen hundreds."

"No kidding? The *Mayflower?*"

Kerry chuckled. "No. From all the people who claim to have ancestors who came over on the *Mayflower*, the ship would have to have been the size of an aircraft carrier."

"I was told my ancestors did," Henry said somewhat stiffly.

"Oh. Well, they probably did." Kerry smothered a smile.

"Anyway, we can use your early New England roots, maybe more than the Irish angle. I visualize some sort of time-travel video, maybe. A colonial costume, very demure, then switch to something ultramodern."

Kerry was glad she hadn't told him about the witch and wondered if Judd would. Their discussions the night before seemed so intimate she couldn't imagine him broadcasting what they'd said, but she still wasn't sure he wouldn't if he could see a way to make a profit from it. She decided to turn the tables on Henry and ask some questions of her own. "How long have you been at Lighthouse?"

"Ever since the name change," Henry said with a proud smile.

"The name change?"

"Used to be called Pegasus Records. Then that business happened with Judd's brother, and Judd changed the name to Lighthouse. I don't know if it was the name change, or knowing he had to take care of Rachel and provide for her future, but the label really took off after that. Judd's probably told you the history."

Kerry sat forward. "Actually, no. We've been so busy there hasn't been time. What happened with his brother?"

"Killed. Drowned, actually."

Kerry put a hand to her mouth.

"He and his wife. Boat smashed on rocks off the coast of Maine. If there'd been a lighthouse, it might have saved them. Judd had one built on that exact spot as soon as he started making big bucks."

Kerry began to understand. "So Rachel isn't his daughter."

"Don't let him ever hear you say that. She's his, all right. Designated her guardian in the will. She was two when it happened, so Judd's her daddy, far as she's concerned." The limo swooped into an alley and pulled up to a dingy back door with an iron gate across it. Henry glanced out the tinted windows. "Here we are. Compulsions."

Kerry was so busy adjusting her picture of Judd that she forgot to be nervous. So Rachel was his adopted daughter. Losing a brother like that would explain the shadows she sometimes saw in his eyes. She wondered what other unprobed depths existed beneath the seemingly calm surface of Judd Roarke. And she wanted to find out.

In the meantime, she had a gig to do. She followed Henry down the dimly lit stairs and through a storeroom crammed with boxes of liquor. Recorded music pounded in from the front of the basement club, signaling the frantic pace of Compulsions. With a name like that, Kerry had expected as much. She'd conferred with Joe, Paul and Woody, who had agreed she should use her most energetic material for Compulsions and save most of her ballads for the Besotted Fox.

Henry reached a heavy brocade curtain that separated the storeroom from the club. "Take a look, get a feel for the place," he said.

Kerry stepped forward and pulled back a small part of the curtain. The room was hazy with smoke. As she watched, the smoke changed colors as rotating spots and flashing strobes created a light show for the couples gyrating on the small dance floor or sitting hip to hip around the ebony cocktail tables. Art deco prints of broad-shouldered, angular men and women, their outlines traced in neon, covered the walls. The night before Kerry had been impressed with the spaciousness of the loft. This low-ceilinged room was a less inspiring venue.

The band was setting up on the stage, which was crammed into one corner. The bar occupied the other front corner, and waitresses with large shoulder pads cantilevered under sleek dresses teetered on four-inch heels as they served trays of drinks. Kerry took heart from watching Woody, Paul and Joe assemble their equipment. She'd only known them two days, but that was longer than she'd known anyone else in the room.

Kerry scanned the crowd, heart pounding, for a face from the night before, since Judd had warned her that a few stars had mentioned they might show up. Would she suddenly be confronted with the sight of Linda Ronstadt or Michael Bolton seated casually at one of the small tables in the back of the room? The lighting and the press of people confused her vision, but after several seconds of panicked surveying, she decided none had shown up, not for this first set, at least.

"What do you think?" Henry murmured, although the recorded music was so loud they couldn't possibly be overheard.

"It's...small."

"Space is a premium in New York. Besides, lots of people like these little places. Consider them cozy, I guess."

Kerry considered them claustrophobic, but she'd never say so, standing here with Henry on the threshold of her career. The road to singing in a huge concert hall began in tiny rooms like this. Intellectually she knew that, but the smoke was already tickling her nose and the back of her throat.

"You stay put," Henry instructed. "There's a powder room to your right, if you need it. I'll tell the band we're here."

Kerry stepped back to let him pass. She imagined the club must be air-conditioned. It would have to be for anyone to survive down there in the summer heat, yet the coolness didn't reach into the alcove where she waited. Her stomach danced an Irish jig, and her makeup felt heavy and ready to slide right off her face.

She tried to think of something to calm her nerves and remembered her tenth birthday when her father had taken her out alone on his fishing boat. It was a ritual all the Muldoon kids had enacted when their age reached double digits, and she was the last. She remembered the fog, and the gentle song of the boat's engine as they'd chugged out to sea. She'd laid her cheek on the rail and thought she even heard words to the song. She couldn't recall them now.

She'd asked her father that day if he thought she'd become famous. "I don't know, lass," he'd said. "Nobody can know that. I just hope you'll be happy."

Henry ducked back through the curtain. "Ready?"

She smoothed her dress with her hands and took a deep breath. "Ready."

JUDD TRIED several things to distract himself as the hour drew near when Kerry would step onto the stage at Compulsions. He tried to finish some paperwork he'd brought home, but he couldn't seem to concentrate. Television had never worked very well as a time filler for him, and it didn't now. As a last resort he put on earphones and cranked up the latest release from Kenny G. His mellow saxophone only made things worse, touching chords in him already sensitized by Kerry's presence in his life.

He had to have something to do. Finally he dug in the back of a closet and dragged out his own saxophone case. Probably couldn't even get a squeak out of the thing, he thought, but at least he'd have a challenge for the next couple of hours.

He assembled the horn with movements that had become habit and would probably remain so. Miracle of miracles, there was an unopened package of reeds stuck in the case. He moistened one in his mouth and fit it into the mouthpiece before lifting the strap over his neck. He was surprised by a rush of excitement as his fingers found the keys and his lips fastened over the mouthpiece. Good thing he was alone; he was about to make a colossal fool of himself.

At first he sounded as bad as he'd expected. The off-key squeaks assaulted his trained ear like fingernails on a chalkboard. But gradually his tone improved, although playing was tough on his lip.

At last he began to settle in and closed his eyes as the music reached inside to a place that hadn't been explored in a long, long time. Not since Steve had died. He hadn't thought about it much, but he hadn't touched the instrument after that. Not that he'd played a lot before the accident, but once in a while—to amuse Michelle and, later, baby Rachel—Steve would haul out his trumpet and Judd would warm up the sax.

Judd played, ignoring the pressure on his uncondi-
tioned lip and his lousy phrasing. How he loved the
sound, loved making the sound. Listening to a sax
didn't hold a candle to playing one. Memories of Suzanne surfaced again, and he realized the pain of losing her had faded into sad regret. Emotions he hadn't
allowed himself to feel found their way out through the
music. Steve's death hammered him, and he found the
courage to play though it, cleansing the dark places,
letting in light. *Yes.*

It was a while before he realized the phone was ring-
ing. Holding the sax, he picked up the cordless phone
on the table behind the sofa. He had to clear his throat
before he could speak. "Roarke."

"Judd, this is Henry. Listen, our girl is struggling."

"Kerry?" His gut twisted. "But—"

"I don't know what it is. The crowd may not be very
good. There can be nights like that. Maybe it's nerves.
But she's not reaching them. Johnson from development and Hammond from artist relations were here and
left. They didn't seem impressed. The atmosphere is
flat."

Judd consulted his watch. He'd lost track of the time
while he played. "You still in the first set?"

"Almost finished."

"I'll come down for the second set, but don't tell her.
I'll stay in the back, out of sight and try to figure out
what's wrong."

"Maybe the second set will go better. I hate to roust
you out, but you said to keep you informed. Is she
someone special to you or something?"

Judd bit back his irritation and kept his tone steady.
"Just promising talent, Henry. We've already spent
some change on her, and I don't want to waste it. I'll be

there in half an hour." He hung up the phone and lifted the saxophone strap over his head. As he laid the instrument back in its case, he decided not to return the case to the back of the closet just yet. Maybe he'd feel like playing again sometime soon.

He caught a cab to Compulsions and tipped the hostess generously to find him a place in the darkest corner of the club. She had to dislodge a passionate couple in order to accomplish that. As the man and woman glared at him, he handed them two hundred dollars and suggested they get a room somewhere. It infuriated him that two people would be groping each other when they should be listening to Kerry sing. If this couple was any indication, Kerry had been handed a bad audience tonight. Sometimes it happened—illogical though it might seem—that nearly everyone in a crowd was a bumblehead.

Kerry came out to lukewarm applause and he ached for her. From last night's triumph to this. As she sang he wanted to go up and haul her off the stage. The crowd was bad, filled with rude people more interested in being stars on the dance floor and comedians at the table than acknowledging talent on the stage.

But Kerry was a little off, too. The sparkle he'd seen each time he'd watched her perform was gone. Technically she wasn't bad, although the indifference of the crowd made her miss a few entrances and bungle the words to one verse of a song. But she persevered, and he saw the mark of the professional in her gritty determination to finish her set, no matter what.

As he sat in the dark, wanting to protect her from the agony of this moment, he remembered all the times he'd played for audiences that couldn't have cared less that he was up there giving them his heart and soul. But it was the nature of performing. Sometimes they loved you, sometimes they hated you and, perhaps worst of all, sometimes they didn't give a shit.

Surely this had happened to Kerry before, but the stakes hadn't been so high. He could read misery in the depths of her green eyes, even from the back of the room.

The forty-five-minute set was pure hell, and he endured it with her. By the end his fists were clenched and he'd barely touched the scotch and soda he'd ordered. As she left the stage, the smattering of applause was almost an insult.

He was out of his seat before she got to the curtain, through the curtain before she was halfway down the hall to the back door. "Kerry!"

She turned, and when she glimpsed him her stoic mask nearly crumbled, as if his presence there made her humiliation complete. But she composed herself and lifted her chin. "Turns out I'm the Blarney stone, after all, Judd," she said in a bravely resonant voice.

At that moment he began to love her.

9

"I DON'T HAPPEN to think so." Judd's voice was the unsteady one. "Thanks for handling this, Henry. I'll take it from here."

Henry, who was escorting Kerry to the car, took one look at Judd's face and stepped aside. "Sure thing. I'll just go back and see how the band's doing. They might need help packing up."

Judd walked toward Kerry. "Zorba's out there?" he asked.

"Henry called him."

For once he was glad Henry had disregarded his policy of not calling the chauffeur late at night. "Then let's go."

"Judd, if you don't mind, I'd rather be alone. As you can imagine, bombing out at a time like this makes people less than sociable, and I—"

"I said let's go." He took her arm and propelled her toward the back door.

"So this is how a CEO gets to behave," she muttered as they walked outside to the waiting gray limo.

"That's right." He handed her inside with a nod at Zorba.

"That's not what you said yesterday." Her green eyes flashed in the dim light from the alley as he climbed in beside her and Zorba put the limo in gear. "You said nobody at Lighthouse gets to be pompous, especially you."

"I'm not going to argue semantics with you, but this isn't being pompous." He glanced up at the front seat. Zorba must be getting a charge out of this conversation. "You took a direct hit tonight, and I'm here for damage control, whether you want me or not." In the confines of the limo, he became aware of the scent of her perfume which was heightened by the heat of the performance and the warmth of a July night. His body tightened in response.

A tremor passed through her. "Whether I want you or not," she murmured, looking away. "My, my. What a difference a day makes, as they say in the old song."

He fought to keep his head. He couldn't act on impulse now. What she needed more than anything else was reassurance of her talent, not a seduction. But God, he wanted her. Now, here in the limo, in the heart of traffic. "Kerry—"

She faced him, eyes brimming. "I don't want your sympathy, okay? If you weren't interested when I was on top of the world, don't come around when I'm sinking out of sight. Let me go away quietly. Or are you here because you want your money's worth, one way or the other?"

With an oath he leaned forward and slammed the window shut between the front seat and the back.

She narrowed her eyes. "Don't want Zorba to know about your baser instincts?"

"It's not like that, dammit!" He was seething with desire, but she couldn't know that, could she? "And you didn't seem to have such a low opinion of me last night in the cab. What was that all about?"

"You tell me." She glared at him through her tears. "You tell me what's going on between us, because I haven't a clue."

He gazed into her eyes and saw it. Lust shimmered beneath the surface of her anger and his. Lust, but also something more delicate, something that might disappear if they turned a white light on it. It disturbed and confused him. For the first time in years he'd hit a crisis he didn't know how to handle. His natural impulses, which he'd followed when he'd kissed her last night, would only get them in more trouble. "I'm sorry," he said at last, feeling frustrated almost beyond endurance.

She swiped at her eyes, smearing her mascara. Then she looked out the window at the stream of cars surrounding them. "No, I'm sorry. I didn't mean to imply you were some lecher. I know you're not. You see, Judd, I wanted to hurt somebody, and you were available."

"You had a bad audience." He wanted to hold her so much his arms ached from the effort to keep them at his sides. "It happens to everyone."

She gripped the armrest and wouldn't look at him. "A good performer can turn an audience around."

"Not always." He clenched his hands to keep from reaching across the short space between them. The headlights of passing cars shone on her glorious hair and sparkled in the crystals at her ears and throat. "Dozens of top performers start out like this, with a miserable night when nothing clicks. The amateurs go home. The pros pick themselves up and go out there again."

He watched the convulsive motion of her throat. She was fighting like a tiger not to cry in front of him.

"You're a pro, Kerry," he said gently.

She turned toward him then. "Not at this moment," she said, tears spilling down her cheeks. "Oh, Judd."

Only a man made of stone wouldn't have opened his arms to such distress. Judd wasn't made of stone. With a sigh he gathered her close and she buried her face against his chest while she cried.

He hated to see her cry, loved that he could hold her while she did. He rested his cheek against her hair and breathed in the wildflower scent of her shampoo. He meant to keep his embrace loose, brotherly, but the longer she stayed in his arms, the firmer his grip became. He had no idea what he said to her as she snuffled against his shirt, but at last she peeked up at him, her eyes red and ringed with mascara.

"You're pretty good at this comforting stuff," she said with a tiny smile.

"Thanks." His heartbeat quickened at the soft look of acceptance in her eyes. Acceptance and something more. A flame was stirring there. Lord help them, a flame was stirring in those emerald eyes.

"I hope you know of a good laundry, or it's the end of the trail for this shirt," she said.

He glanced down at the white silk Armani. The fabric was stained with her tears and stage makeup that might never wash out. "It's only a shirt," he said, keeping his arms firmly around her.

"I guess it's better that I sacrificed your shirt, instead of this dress. It has to last me through the week."

He felt dizzy, as if they were being propelled toward an inevitable conclusion. Maybe he was a fool to resist. "Then you're staying?"

"Must be that stubborn Irish blood."

"I guess so," he said, his voice husky. He thought of her admission that she'd come to New York with one cocktail dress to her name, one outfit to conquer the city that was a primary fashion mecca. Her vulnerability wrenched his heart. But if anyone could pull off a coup like that, it was Kerry.

"The car's not moving anymore," she said.

"No." He watched the flame in her eyes grow stronger.

"I guess that means we're at the Salisbury."

"Yes." He didn't loosen his grip. Somehow he couldn't conceive of getting out of this car and telling her good-night at the door. Not after her tears. Not after her bravery. He couldn't douse the flame that beckoned him closer, closer. What he was thinking was dangerous for him, perhaps for her, too. But he couldn't send her away tonight.

There was a button on the armrest that activated an intercom. Holding her with one arm, he reached over and pushed the button. "Zorba?"

"Yes, Mr. Roarke."

"Take us to my apartment."

KERRY'S GAZE snapped up to his face. There she found the intensity that had lurked in his eyes from the first day she'd seen him. She had no doubt why they were going to his apartment.

Maybe she was naive, and this was the music-industry version of the casting couch. But she didn't believe it, despite the accusation she'd flung at him in the heat of her frustration over her performance tonight. She believed that Judd was a good and honorable man.

She held his gaze, chest tight with anticipation, as the limo whizzed through the night.

When the car stopped on Central Park West and she realized she'd soon be walking in front of the apartment building's doorman, she started to struggle in his arms. "I'm a mess. Let me—"

"You're beautiful." He held her fast until she felt bathed in the sensuous warmth that radiated from him. Suddenly she no longer cared about her smudged makeup or her red-rimmed eyes. To bask in this powerful radiance, if only for one night, would be worth whatever price she had to pay. Maybe she'd end up with a broken heart. But maybe she'd end up with the glass slipper.

Zorba's expression was unreadable as he opened the car door for them. The doorman, too, showed no expression as Judd guided her through the revolving doors into the lobby.

She and Judd didn't speak as they rode alone in the subdued elegance of the elevator. He held her hand loosely, his thumb circling lazily against her palm, his gaze fixed on her. She knew that later they might talk, but for now, words would only get in the way.

What they were about to do made no logical sense, but they were doing it, anyway. If they spoke, they might decide to take a more prudent path, but with the blood rushing through her veins in response to his simple caress, she wouldn't seek a more prudent path. His leisurely touch reminded her of his long, supple fingers that she'd admired once on a sunny day in Eternity. Perhaps she'd known, even then, that one day those supple fingers would prove their artistry on her body.

He let her into the apartment where soft lights were burning, lights he must have left on when he rushed off to rescue her. He led her through a foyer carpeted with an oriental rug into a living room decorated in rich tones of plum and moss. Despite the intrusion of the ever-present traffic noises of New York, the room seemed hushed and private, like a sanctuary.

She noticed a leather instrument case on the lacquered coffee table and started to ask about it, but he pulled her to him and cupped her face in his hands.

The hard planes of his chiseled features seemed almost fierce as he drew a shaky breath. "Last chance to back out."

She lifted her face to his. "I need you."

"I'm here." His lips hovered near, tasted, withdrew, tasted again. His fingers worked up through her hair, releasing the pins, combing her hair down around her shoulders while his mouth explored and savored hers. *He kisses like a musician*, she thought before those kisses sent her mind spinning away from rational thought.

They left her dress in a scarlet splash in the middle of the living room, his makeup-stained shirt in the hall, their shoes at the bedroom door. Judd fumbled with a light switch and a small bedside lamp spilled a pool of light that illuminated a walnut four-poster bed covered in a moss-and-blue comforter. Kerry thought fleetingly of her disheveled appearance and reached over his shoulder to flip the switch off.

Judd laughed softly and kissed her while he turned it back on. "I want to see you sparkle," he murmured against her mouth.

She had no more say in the matter as he urged her backward until they reached the bed and she tumbled onto the fluffy comforter. Then she forgot about the light as he slipped down beside her and seemed to kiss her underwear away. In easy, sensuous motions he left her wearing nothing but her crystal necklace and earrings.

His touch was like music, one caress flowing into another, each building toward a melody that was excitingly new, yet hauntingly familiar. As he kissed her breasts, her nipples, the insides of her thighs, she had the wild feeling she'd become a musical instrument. And not just any instrument, but one of superb quality, a Stradivarius vibrating with a richness she hadn't known she possessed. She grew taut as harp strings, resonant as the tight skin of a drum.

How he played her!

Fingertips pressing, mouth slipping easily over her damp skin, he pushed her to greater heights of sensation with each fresh assault. She arched as he found the heated core of her with his fingers, gasped when he put his mouth there. She gave him her sighs of delight, her moans of ecstasy and finally, in a burst of joy, her cries of completion.

Then he was beside her again, stroking and kissing her back to arousal once more. She wanted more, and he had more to give. A brief moment away from her, and he returned. She rubbed her hands over his sweat-dampened chest where glistening drops of moisture clung to the wiry hair. She gazed into his tawny eyes and saw her own passion reflected there.

He moved over her and braced his arms on either side of her head. He was breathing hard and she could sense the superhuman control that allowed him to enter her gently, slowly, watching her eyes as he filled her.

She lifted her hips to meet him. His nostrils flared and he shoved deeper, his first impatient gesture of the night.

"Yes," she said, her voice husky from the effects of his lovemaking. She rotated her hips and watched in satisfaction as his eyes closed.

He opened his eyes, withdrew and entered her again, more forcefully this time. She pushed upward, meeting his thrust. With a growl of pleasure he cupped her behind, and this time he buried himself in her without holding back.

She gripped his shoulders and held on as he pushed her relentlessly toward another climax, but this time she gazed into his eyes, determined to watch the crescendo building in him, too.

He took her there first, and her vision blurred as she whirled in the heart of the maelstrom. He followed soon afterward with a shout of triumph that echoed through her fevered brain in a final drumroll of passion.

In the dazed aftermath, as he rested his forehead against hers and their glistening bodies settled together in sweet juxtaposition, she understood for the first time why some women mated for life, why they couldn't love another, even if they tried. It was this that bound them, this perfection of union that would be a travesty to even try and duplicate.

Had he felt it, too? For the sake of her heart, she prayed that he had.

His breath was warm against her ear. "Don't go away," he whispered, and eased from the bed. In a moment he was back, cradling her in his arms, smoothing the tangled hair from her face. "You need to know something."

She gazed into his eyes. She needed to know everything, but would he choose to tell her?

"This isn't the way I usually operate."

That made her smile. "Then I think you've really hit upon something."

He smiled back. "I meant that I don't bring women here."

"What does that make me?"

His eyes sparkled. "Most probably a witch. But I just didn't want you to think that I was exactly the kind of man you imagined when you were talking to the gulls that morning. Somebody who dumped his daughter for the summer so he could live it up while she was gone."

She touched his cheek. "Do you care what I think?"

"As it happens, I do."

"That's nice."

"I don't know about that." His gaze was warm. "My feelings for you could turn out to be a real problem for both of us."

She ran her hand over his hip. "Is making love with the CEO against company policy?"

"Mostly against my personal policy. Business is supposed to be strictly business."

"I see." The devil in her guided her hand to his groin, where she fondled him intimately.

His eyes darkened. "But you refuse to be put in a neat compartment."

"*We* can't be put in a neat compartment." She wrapped her fingers around his stiffening shaft. "Even if you are the CEO and I'm the potential client, we've been striking sparks off each other from the day we met."

He groaned and closed his eyes. "But you're headed for fame and fortune. You don't need this."

"And what about you?" She slid her hand away.

"I . . ."

She leaned down and took him in her mouth.

"I need this," he gasped. "Oh, Kerry, I need this."

10

KERRY AWOKE the next morning to find herself alone in the big four-poster. She stretched slowly and marveled at how wonderful she felt, considering she'd had one of the most miserable performances of her life the night before. But after Judd's lovemaking, the performance seemed unimportant.

She glanced around the room for clues to his personality. Apparently he liked dark woods and rich, muted colors. A desk beneath the window had some papers strewn on it; a leather briefcase sat on the floor next to the wooden swivel chair. Framed pictures of Rachel at various ages were scattered throughout the room—on the desk, the walnut dresser, the bedside table. A few pictures of a young couple with a toddler were also mixed in. Rachel and her parents. Kerry was touched that Judd kept these reminders so close at hand.

As for his taste in art, his erotic nature was highlighted in his choice of lush landscapes with trees in full foliage covering sensuously rolling hills. Or perhaps after last night's experience with Judd she was reading more into the paintings.

In the height of passion, he was ravenous, but in quieter moments she could tell he wasn't completely comfortable with their new status as lovers. He'd tried a few more times during the night to discuss why they might be making a mistake, but then he'd reach for her, or she'd reach for him, and they'd be immersed in the wonder they created together simply by touching.

She decided he might be the kind of man who needed a while to get used to an idea. If he didn't want his associates to know about their liaison, she'd keep it secret until it no longer mattered. Once she'd earned a measure of fame, their love affair wouldn't be much of a scandal. It might not be one now, but she'd defer to Judd on that score. This was his backyard she was playing in, after all. And, boy, had they played!

An antique wall clock pointed to a little after seven. Traffic was already bustling on the street below, but inside the apartment silence reigned, except for the ticking of the clock. She didn't think Judd would leave her here alone, but she didn't know all aspects of his personality yet.

She climbed out of bed and padded into a bathroom scented with soap and shaving cream. Moisture still clung to the pebbled shower door. She must have been exhausted to have slept through his morning routine. She washed her face and ran her fingers through her hair, wincing as she encountered tangles. A wine-colored terry robe hung on a hook behind the bathroom door. She put it on and went in search of its owner.

Halfway down the hall she heard Judd's voice and paused. If he had visitors she didn't want to be seen. Soon she recognized a one-sided conversation that indicated he was on the telephone. He laughed, and her heart lurched with pleasure.

Following the scent of fresh-brewed coffee, she continued down the hall and into the living room. From there she could see him sitting in the kitchen at a butcher-block table, a cordless phone to his ear and his fingers crooked through the handle of a maroon coffee mug. He hadn't seen her yet, and she took the opportunity to study him.

He wore dark slacks and a fresh white silk shirt with a red-and-navy-striped tie expertly knotted at his throat. Gold cuff links gleamed at each wrist, and a gold watch flashed when he pulled back one cuff to check the time. He'd propped his ankle on his knee, revealing black wing tips that had been buffed until they glowed.

He seemed to be enjoying the conversation. His tone was light and teasing, his smile quick to appear at something said on the other end of the line. Kerry gazed at him with a mixture of affection and desire that she realized could easily deepen to something more permanent. Until she understood his heart, she'd have to be cautious to protect her own.

She walked forward and he glanced up. His smile faded and the sparkle of light humor left his eyes. His gaze searched hers as she walked toward him.

"Well, time for me to get to work, punkin," he said. "Say hi to Grandma and Grandpa.... Okay. Talk to you tomorrow." He snapped off the phone and put it on the table next to his coffee cup. "Good morning," he said in an even tone. Questions lurked in his eyes. "Coffee?"

"I'll get it." She moved to the coffeemaker, where a second mug sat, and poured herself a cup. "That was Rachel?" she asked, her back to him.

"I call her in the morning."

She turned, the warm mug to her lips. "Every morning?"

"Yes."

"What a loving thing to do."

He stood and came toward her. "She's important to me."

"I could tell from the way you talked to her." Kerry cradled the mug in both hands, glad to have a prop as they felt their way back to the ease they'd enjoyed the night before. "She's lucky to have you."

"I'm lucky to have her." He paused a few feet from her and they studied each other for a long moment.

"I don't know what to do next," she said softly. "You look so . . . *dressed*."

"To hell with that." He took one stride forward and took the mug from her hand. He set it on the counter behind her and drew her into his arms.

She sighed and slid her hands up his back, over the smooth expanse of silk. "Mornings after are so tough."

"I thought you might wake up with regrets," he murmured against her temple.

"No." She nestled closer, inhaling the crisp scent of his after-shave. "You?"

"No. I have no idea how this will work out, but I'll never regret what happened between us last night." He pushed her hair aside and kissed her neck. "When I saw you standing there looking like a woman who'd been making love all night, I wanted to turn the clock back and start all over." He nipped gently at her throat and she arched against him in response.

"But the clock ticks on," she murmured.

"Unfortunately." He lifted his head and gazed down at her. "And we have some decisions to make."

"I don't eat breakfast. Coffee's fine."

"Bigger decisions than that."

Her stomach churned. She'd rather drift a while, but this man wasn't a drifter. "Okay."

"Or we could avoid decisions and play coy little games."

"Such as?"

"I could send you home in a cab, and then tonight after we inevitably end up at your hotel to make love, I'd go home in a cab, and so on, each of us pretending we're acting on impulse."

She waited, wondering if this would be his noble speech about ending the relationship now before they became too involved. She was already too involved.

"Or you could move in here for the rest of the time you're in New York."

She caught her breath.

"If you think the pressure would be too great—living with me—I'd understand. I'm not attaching strings to this, for either of us. I just want you close."

"Would anyone know?"

"That's up to you."

She realized the gift he'd just given her. If she chose to broadcast their relationship, he'd endure whatever insinuations came his way. But the insinuations would hurt her more than they would him. "Do you think . . . Should I consider going to another record company?"

His gaze was steady. "That's also up to you. I compromised our business relationship last night. I know that, and I'll accept the consequences. If you're uncomfortable with Lighthouse and want to try another company, I won't stop you."

"I don't want another company." She smiled. "Besides, I don't feel the least bit compromised."

A roguish look came into his eyes. "Then maybe I didn't do it right." He reached to loosen the belt holding the robe together.

"Judd." She squirmed away from him, although the look in his eyes brought desire rushing back. "You're all ready for work, and I need a shower."

"All right." He stepped forward, and before she understood his purpose, he'd swept her into his arms. The robe gaped open as he carried her down the hall, through the bedroom and into the bathroom.

"What in—?" Her question ended in a shriek as he carried her into the spacious shower. In swift succession he put her down, shut the glass door and turned the water on full blast. "Your robe! Your clothes!" she cried. Then she couldn't speak as he closed her mouth with a heated kiss.

Gently he pushed the sodden robe from her shoulders. "Undress me, Kerry," he murmured, licking drops of water from her cheeks.

The warm water pulsed over her shoulders and streamed down her breasts as she loosened the soggy knot of his tie. "It's ruined," she whispered, pulling it free and glancing up at him through water-spiked lashes.

"Damn things are useless, anyway. Except perhaps for this." He looped the wet tie around her waist and drew her close, dipping his head to sip at each breast as water sluiced over the textured surface of her nipples.

She looked at him through eyes heavy lidded with passion. "Your shirt's soaked, too."

He straightened and brought the tie down, rubbing it lazily across her buttocks. "Then take it off."

The soft friction of the silk tie against her skin was incredibly arousing. Forcing herself to concentrate on the task he'd given her, she unbuttoned his shirt, transparent now and plastered to his chest. She peeled it back from one nipple and flicked her tongue over the hard peak. With her palm pressed against his heart to feel its rapid thrumming, she stripped away the other side of the shirt and repeated the gesture. Then she kissed and nibbled until his breathing grew ragged.

"Very nice," he said, his voice husky.

He held his hands still when she reached to unfasten each cuff link. Then he had to drop one end of the tie as she pulled the shirtsleeve over his hand. He retrieved it from between her legs, and when the silk slipped across her aroused femininity, she gave a small gasp.

Looking into her eyes, he drew the tie slowly back between her thighs. "I think I've found another use for this tie," he murmured. Then he pulled the front end forward, slowly parting the delicate petals of her femininity with the damp silk. She cried out softly as the sensation shot through her. He pulled the silk back, then forward again as she moaned in reaction. Satisfaction gleamed in his eyes, and he captured her lips with his own as he continued to move the tie lazily back and forth.

The tender touch, so easy yet softly persistent, caught her by surprise. Her knees grew weak and she leaned against the shower wall.

"Good?" he whispered, cinching the loop a little tighter.

Her sigh was the only answer he seemed to need as he gradually increased the pressure. The tension mounted until finally she gripped his shoulders for balance as she began to lose control. Gasping, she closed her eyes and gave herself up to a shattering climax.

Dropping the tie to the floor of the shower, he kissed her eyelids and ran his tongue over her parted lips as he held her close. "I'll never call those things useless again," he whispered.

Gradually sanity returned. She would repay him in kind. She opened her eyes and found the answering fire in his. "I don't think we're quite finished with this shower," she murmured, unbuckling his belt and drawing the zipper down. His underwear, too, was soaked, and when she uncovered the firmness of his erection, she was surprised the briefs weren't steaming. Kneeling in the pounding spray, she kissed him there and reveled in his intake of breath. She pulled off his shoes and stripped off his socks. He kicked away the last of his clothes.

The water coursed over them and she followed its trail with her tongue down his muscled calves and behind his knees. He began to tremble as her kisses charted the flat plane of his stomach and moved lower. She tasted the salty magnificence of him and he groaned deep in his throat.

With water-slicked fingers and playful tongue she commanded his response and drove him slowly insane. Finally, palms braced against the glass shower wall, he surrendered to her assault as her name escaped his lips in a hoarse cry.

JUDD WAS NEVER LATE for work. Today he was, but that was the least of his worries. He strode past Lois and asked her to hold his calls for half an hour. He needed time to think.

Gazing out his window at Rockefeller Center, he wondered what the hell he thought he was doing, moving Kerry in with him while she was in New York. And the deed was done. By now a trusted employee at the Salisbury had packed her things and sent them via

Zorba over to his apartment. She was probably dressing now, preparing to come to the studio. But he'd take care to avoid her. They'd decided on that course, at least.

Hell. He paced in front of the window and flexed his fingers. He didn't want to face what he was thinking. It was unworthy of him. But ever since last night, when she'd bombed at Compulsions, an evil little voice had been whispering inside his head.

The voice said Kerry might fail.

Maybe he'd been wrong when he'd imagined star quality in her. Maybe he'd been so smitten by her in Eternity that he'd misjudged her audience appeal. Sure, she'd charmed the crowd on Fourth of July. They were primed for it. And as for Monday night at the reception, just about everyone there had looked at Kerry and seen themselves as young hopefuls. Of course they'd cheered her on.

But the crowd at Compulsions was the real test, and she hadn't moved them. Was he that much of a cad that he was banking on her failure? Was he binding her to him sexually so he'd still have some hold on her when he had to deliver the bad news that she wasn't cut out for the big time?

No.

If that had been part of his thinking, he'd squash that motivation now. Kerry wanted fame, and he'd do whatever he could to give it to her. She cared for him, and he could provide a base of support when she desperately needed one. Without him there last night she would have gone back to Eternity. He'd prevented that, and he could cushion whatever other blows came her way while she was here. With his help, she'd make it.

And that would cost him. She'd unlocked emotions he hadn't felt since...since Suzanne. He'd always wondered if he'd ever love with that sort of intensity again. He had his answer. He could love even more intensely. Last night had been incredible, and this morning... He hadn't pulled an insane stunt like that in fifteen years. Feeling wild and carefree, heedless of the consequences, was terrific while it lasted, but there was always a price to pay, wasn't there? Look at Suzanne. Look at Steve.

Two people in Judd's life had brought out the uninhibited, joyous side of him. Both of those people were dead. Now here was a third person who made him ignore caution and live for the moment. He wasn't morbid enough to think Kerry would die, too. But she'd leave him, which for him would have the same consequence.

She needed him now, but when the applause started coming again, she wouldn't. He could picture the guilt and sorrow in her green eyes as she told him she had to move on. Then there'd be the wrenching in his gut as he let her go.

But until that day came, she needed his support, his encouragement, even his love. In offering all that to her, he was probably as crazy as Steve had been, sailing his catamaran out of the harbor despite the storm clouds on the horizon. Maybe he and Steve weren't so different, after all.

His phone buzzed and he glanced at his watch. Good thing it was waterproof, although after what happened in the shower this morning, he wouldn't have cared if the expensive works had rusted beyond repair.

Unfortunately his half hour of thinking time had elapsed. With a sigh he punched a button and picked up the receiver.

"Stella Woodhouse is on the line," Lois said. "Shall I take a message or put her through?"

"Put her through." He had to subdue a moment of panic whenever he got a call from Stella. There was always the possibility something had happened to Rachel. He cleared the tension from his throat and picked up the phone. "Hi, Stella."

"Hi, Judd. Rachel's fine."

He released his held breath. He appreciated her starting out that way. She was a good person, which made his decision all the more difficult. "Glad to hear it."

"I hate to bother you at work, but I wanted to call you when Rachel isn't around. She's just gone over to Marcie's house to play."

"That's okay, Stella. I've told you to call anytime. Rachel's my top priority."

"I realize that. I'm sure you've given a lot of thought to our discussion the night of the clambake. I took Rachel over to the school today, and she seemed to like it. The teacher she would have for fifth grade happened to be there. Mrs. Bierce. She and Rachel really hit it off."

"I see." The campaign was continuing. Judd sat back in his swivel chair and massaged his temple where a headache threatened. "Did you ask Rachel if she'd like to go to school there?"

"Well, no, not specifically. I wouldn't put that kind of question to her unless I knew what you'd decided. That's why I'm calling, to find out if you have decided anything."

"No. No, I haven't." The pain moved to the back of his head.

"I don't want to push you, Judd, but if we're going to do this . . ."

"I know. Give me a week, Stella."

There was a brief hesitation on the other end of the line. "Are you . . . seeing someone?"

He wanted to laugh. Stella was afraid he'd found a candidate for a wife, which would end the Woodhouses' chances of keeping Rachel. If Stella only knew the circumstances of the woman he was "seeing," she wouldn't worry at all.

"Never mind," she said quickly when he didn't answer. "I didn't mean to pry."

"I just need more time. I'm sorry to keep you hanging like this, but there are so many things to consider."

"I understand. A week is fine. That will give us plenty of time before school starts. Take care, Judd. I'll talk to you in a week."

"Goodbye, Stella." He hung up the phone and rubbed the back of his neck. He'd been expecting her call, and he should have made up his mind by now. Except Kerry had occupied his thoughts so completely that he'd pushed the matter of Rachel's future to the back of his mind.

Until last night he'd kidded himself that some wonderful woman might show up and solve his problems. The wonderful woman had shown up, and his problems were greater than ever. He'd been around enough to know that he wouldn't easily find someone as perfect for him as Kerry. But Kerry wasn't aiming for the job of wife and mother, and Rachel's needs couldn't be put on hold much longer.

Judd swiveled his chair and gazed unseeingly at the magnificent view from his office window. Rachel and Kerry were the two people who made his life worth living. And if he kept their interests in mind, instead of his own, there was a good chance he'd end up losing them both.

11

THAT NIGHT Kerry sang for Judd. The rest of the crowd didn't matter to her. She thought the response she got was better than the night before, but there were still people in the audience she never reached. She ignored them and focused on Judd. Although he sat in the back of the room and she couldn't see his face well, she used her memories of him to fill in what the shadows obscured. He was her lifeline.

No matter what happened with this audience, she'd be in Judd's arms at the end of the night. He believed in her, cared for her, and satisfied longings she hadn't known she had. During taping and rehearsals that day she'd been caught staring off into space a few times, but other than that she thought she'd hid her preoccupation with Judd quite well.

Toward the end of the last set she grew impatient to be with him again. The crowd had thinned, and cigarette smoke had made her throat raw. When she finally took her last bow to a smattering of applause, she fled the stage and nearly ran down the hall to the back door, where Judd would be waiting in the limo.

Zorba stood holding the car door open, and she practically threw herself into the limo and Judd's arms.

"Finally," she breathed against his questing mouth.

He kissed her thoroughly before drawing back. "Tonight went better," he murmured.

"Yes." She traced the outline of his mouth and used her thumb to wipe away the smudges of lipstick she'd left there. "I've probably been expecting too much. A nightclub audience in New York won't respond like a wedding-reception crowd in Eternity."

"No."

"Oh, Judd, I—" She paused and glanced at the window separating them from Zorba. It was closed. She turned to him and grinned. "I've missed you like crazy."

"Same here." He gazed into her eyes. "It's a wonder I got anything done today."

"Do you think anyone has guessed?"

"If they have, they're not saying."

She glanced toward the front of the limo again. "What about Zorba?"

"Someone could drive splinters under his fingernails and he wouldn't talk about my private business."

"Really?"

"Really." He cupped her chin and lowered his mouth to hers. This time she was delighted when the limo hurtled forward. She was in a hurry.

She and Judd barely made it through his front door before they began tearing at each other's clothes. Kerry heard a seam give way beneath her arm.

Judd heard it, too, and paused. "Your dress."

"I can mend it." Her fingers flew over the buttons of his shirt. "Just love me, Judd."

"I've been waiting all day to hear you say that." His sure fingers divested her of the red dress and cupped her breasts, bringing them to his waiting mouth.

She'd only unbuckled his belt by the time he guided her, wet and pulsing, to the deep pile of the living room rug.

He braced himself on his knees and one palm. "You've turned me into a madman," he gasped, ripping down his zipper and yanking at his briefs to reveal a thrusting erection.

"I like madmen." She reached down and caressed him, her heart pounding in anticipation.

He fumbled in the pocket of his slacks, which still hung around his hips, and pulled out a condom.

"You keep those in your pocket now?"

"Depraved, isn't it?"

"No," she murmured.

"I even thought about making love in the limo." He struggled with the cellophane. "But the window tint isn't dark enough."

She took the package from him. "Let me."

He relinquished it and remained braced over her, breathing hard, while she lovingly sheathed him. "God, hurry," he begged.

"But I love touching you."

He groaned.

She smoothed the latex down, regretting that she was covering his glorious satin skin. She wanted him, unprotected, deep inside her, his essence flowing into her. She wanted it in a primal way that made her mouth moisten and her fingers tremble. She could strip away the condom and seduce him. He was gradually losing all rational thought, and he wouldn't stop.

"Kerry." His voice was hoarse.

She looked up into his eyes. No, not yet. Maybe not ever. After all, they'd said nothing about love. With one last caress, she leaned back and raised her hips in silent invitation. He made a noise low in his throat and thrust home. She closed her eyes and savored the press of him deep inside her. She had this much. She shouldn't be greedy for more.

THE NEXT MORNING Kerry awoke to find Judd sitting on the end of the bed, dressed in the burgundy robe and examining her red dress.

Still naked, but with the comforter tucked up under her arms, she propped herself up on one elbow and pushed the hair from her eyes. "Don't tell me you sew, too?"

He glanced over his shoulder and smiled. "Nope. Not one of my talents. This dress needs more than one seam repaired, though."

"I'll see what I can do."

"Don't worry about it." He stood and laid the dress over the back of his desk chair. "We'll send it out to be cleaned and mended today."

"But I—"

"In fact, we're going one step further. I need to buy you another dress. I should be able to get away for an hour or so. I'll meet you somewhere and we'll pick something out."

She flushed. "Judd, you shouldn't do that. I don't expect Lighthouse to buy my—"

"I didn't say Lighthouse is buying it. I am."

"That's even worse. As if I'm some sort of kept woman."

His tawny eyes darkened as he crossed to the bed and grasped her bare arms. "Is that what you think? That you're going to owe me something after this?"

She was taken aback by the fierceness of his gaze. "Well, after all, you—"

"No." His fingers tightened on her arms. "You owe me nothing. Not now or ever. I brought you to New

York because I thought you might make money for my company. Strictly business."

She met his gaze, her heart pounding. "And what is this?"

His grip softened and he settled her gently to the bed again. "Pleasure," he murmured. "And I hope to hell that's what it is for you, because if I thought you were in this bed out of some sense of obligation, I'd—"

She laughed then, thinking of the pounding need that engulfed her whenever they touched, a need that even now was curling through her, begging to be satisfied. "Obligation?" she said. "I don't think so."

"Good," he murmured, running his fingers lightly up her arms. "Then we'll get the dress today during a lunch break. We're not far from Saks."

She hooked a finger through the tie of his robe and pulled gently. "Okay."

A smile twitched at the corners of his mouth. "If I hadn't been mauling you the past two nights your red one would be in better shape. I knew it was all you had and I should have been more careful."

She pulled the belt free and his robe fell open. She feasted on the sight of his aroused body. "You don't ever have to apologize for being anxious to get my clothes off."

He threw back the covers and gazed at her, his eyes taking in her breasts as they quivered from her rapid breathing. "Then maybe I'll buy you several dresses, so I can rip them off you. God, but you're glorious, Kerry."

She smiled up at him. "Maybe I should sing dressed like this."

He shrugged out of the robe. "Only for me," he murmured, lowering himself down beside her and circling her nipple with his tongue. "Only for me," he whispered again, and groaned as he took it in his mouth.

KERRY STOOD before a triple mirror in a dressing room at Saks Fifth Avenue as a solicitous saleswoman adjusted the thin strap of the fourth dress Kerry had tried on so far. The first three had been chosen by her and the saleswoman. This last one had been selected by Judd. He sat in an upholstered chair just outside the dressing room door, his ankle crossed over his knee, his tie loosened. From the moment they'd entered the store, he'd seemed perfectly at ease with the idea of picking out Kerry's dress.

Apparently he knew exactly what he wanted to see, because as soon as she'd appeared in the other three dresses, he'd given one quick shake of his head.

On the third one she'd decided to argue with him. She liked the emerald green, which went well with her eyes. And a glimpse at the price tag told her the dress was the least expensive of the four. It would do fine, and she wouldn't feel so guilty about the gift. True, the green dress had long, unfashionable puffed sleeves and an unfortunate white silk rose at the waist, but it would suffice.

"We can remove the rose," the saleswoman had said, fluttering around Kerry. "We might even be able to take in the sleeves a bit, although I'm not sure that wouldn't defeat the design."

"And we can cut her hair so she'll look like Julie Andrews in *The Sound of Music*. Nope. I know what I'm looking for."

"I think you're being too picky," Kerry had offered.

He'd regarded her calmly. "I've been told that, too. Try the black."

She'd saved the black dress for last, because it cost more than six months' worth of income from her piano students. Black stretch lace sprinkled with rhinestones scooped low over her breasts and hugged her waist and hips to the top of her thighs. Where the body-molding lace ended, the skirt continued in a swirl of sheer black chiffon that ended at midcalf. Judd had picked out rhinestone-studded sling-backed pumps to go with it.

Kerry turned in front of the mirror. The folds of chiffon twirled, providing glimpses of her legs through the material. The black lace outlined her breasts and accentuated her small waist. It was a dress made for seduction. Taking a deep breath, she walked out of the dressing room.

Judd didn't change position when she appeared, but she saw his jaw tighten. A light came into his eyes. It was a look she'd learned to know in the past two days, and her heart quickened.

"Isn't she lovely?" the saleswoman gushed. "You have exquisite taste, Mr. Roarke. Exquisite."

Judd didn't say anything, but there was no quick shake of the head this time. Kerry turned slowly, enjoying her sense of power. She'd struck him dumb. It wasn't every day a girl could do that to a man as experienced as Judd Roarke. She paused as the skirt swirled back into place. "Well?"

"Nice." His voice sounded strained, and he shifted his weight ever so slightly in the chair. She wondered if his briefs were becoming a little tight.

"It's very expensive," she said.

"But considering the workmanship," the saleswoman said, "and that the designer is so well-known, and considering how wonderful the dress looks on her, I think it's a bargain."

Judd didn't say anything, just kept looking at Kerry.

"I wasn't sure if you noticed the price tag when you picked it out," Kerry ventured.

"I did. Get it."

She hesitated.

"Please."

She heard more than courtesy in his tone. He was fast becoming a desperate man. "All right," she said, and left for the dressing room.

As soon as she was out of the dress the saleswoman whisked it away. "Mr. Roarke says he'll pay for this now. Apparently he's late for an appointment."

Kerry glanced at her watch as she put on her blouse. She knew Judd had blocked out an hour for this shopping trip, and they'd only been gone from the office for half that time. She stepped into her skirt and buttoned it quickly, wondering what had come up.

When she emerged from the dressing room Judd was standing there, the dress in a garment bag slung over one shoulder. "Let's go."

"Aren't we going back separately? You can give me the dress and leave if you have an appointment."

"I've changed my mind about going back separately."

"Okay." She hurried to keep up with his long strides as he left the store and stepped into the hot humid air outside.

He glanced behind him to see if she was there before moving to the curb and giving a sharp whistle. Kerry marveled when a taxi swung to the curb immediately. She should take taxi-hailing lessons from this man. When he was in a hurry, he knew what to do.

When he leaned forward and gave the driver his home address, Kerry began to understand what the hurry was.

"I thought you had an important appointment?" she asked, giving him an innocent look.

"I do." He tugged off his tie and stuffed it in his jacket pocket.

"I see." Kerry smiled and leaned back against the seat.

The ride in the cab was fast and furious. Judd's lovemaking in the apartment was very similar, but Kerry wasn't complaining.

"I don't want to go back to the office," he admitted as they lay entwined on his bed.

"Then stay here. Play your saxophone for me."

He lifted his head and looked at her.

"I didn't mess with it, just unlatched the cover and peeked in. I thought you said you didn't play anymore?"

"I didn't." He stroked her cheek with his knuckles. "Until you came along. Then it seemed just the thing to do."

"Then do it now. I'd love to hear you."

He gave her a lopsided grin and bounded off the bed. "Sorry, gotta run."

"My goodness, you're too shy to play for me."

"Of course not. I'm too busy." He headed for the shower.

She followed him. "I don't believe you. I think you're ducking out."

"Nope." He spoke over the roar of the shower. "Got a meeting in half an hour."

"Which I had the feeling you were ready to cancel a moment ago, before I mentioned the sax."

"Change the middle letter of that word and we'll talk."

"But I really want to hear you play."

He turned off the shower, stepped out and reached behind her for a towel. "Maybe some other time."

"Like when?" She followed him into the bedroom. "How about tonight after my gig?"

He threw the towel down and opened a drawer to take out a clean pair of briefs. "Considering what you'll be wearing tonight for your performance, I hardly think I'll be in the mood to play my saxophone."

She leaned close and batted her eyes at him. "I adore a man who plays a saxophone, Judd."

"You only adore a man who plays it well." He shoved his arms into the sleeves of a clean shirt and fastened his cuff links. "I don't. At least not anymore."

"I don't believe you."

"Believe me." He dropped a quick kiss on her lips before continuing to dress with quick efficient movements. "I'll take a cab to the office. Why don't you follow me in about fifteen minutes? I'm sure the band wants to go over a few things before tonight. And Tom, the producer, wants a crack at recording some of the songs you're performing at Compulsions. He really wants you to make it."

"That's nice."

"And so do I." He buckled his belt and grabbed his jacket from the back of the desk chair where he'd tossed it. "See you after your last set. And make sure the zipper on that dress works." He kissed her once more, fast and hard, before leaving the room.

Kerry sank onto the edge of the bed with a sigh. Life sure moved at a frantic pace in New York. Being with Judd was wonderful, but she missed her morning walks on the beach and the lunch hours she'd often spend on Soldier's Green with a sandwich and a can of soda. Since she'd arrived in New York she hadn't seen much daylight except briefly in the morning before she started work at the studio.

She stood and went over to touch a philodendron in the corner of Judd's bedroom. To her surprise it was silk. Very realistic silk, but silk nevertheless. Putting on her robe, which now hung next to his on the bathroom door, she made a quick tour of the apartment. Every plant in it was fake.

She thought about that while she showered and dressed. As she stepped into the muggy heat outside, she glanced with longing across the street toward Central Park. She'd never thought much about needing green things around her. She'd just always had them, and now she didn't. You could stroll in Central Park—there was even a song that said so.

The doorman would have called her a cab, but Kerry was determined to flag one down herself. She walked a block away from the apartment building and started signaling as cabs whizzed by. Maybe she'd have to learn to whistle through her teeth the way Judd did. Twice someone beat her out, but finally she jumped in ahead of another would-be taxi stealer.

Unfortunately the air-conditioning didn't work well in the one she'd caught. She rolled down a window and was greeted with the stench of exhaust.

"I think we're having one of them inversions," the driver said.

"No doubt." Kerry thought again of Central Park. Maybe tomorrow she'd beg off for a couple of hours and walk through it. She needed grass and trees. She'd like a little ocean, too, but the grass and trees would do for now. And she wanted to hear Judd play the sax. For some reason, that had become very important to her.

She remembered how he'd looked at her when she'd first walked out of the dressing room in the black dress. She smiled. A man who looked at a woman like that could be convinced to do just about anything. Even play the sax.

12

THAT NIGHT a few of the celebrities from Monday night's party showed up at Compulsions, and Kerry was grateful for the black dress. Now they wouldn't see her in the same thing she'd worn to the benefit. After the first set, while Kerry sat with Judd and sipped mineral water, several people came over to offer her congratulations on the performance, and Kerry listened in a kind of daze.

"And the dress is dynamite," a woman commented before leaving the table.

Kerry turned to Judd. "Thank you."

He smiled. "Business investment."

"You said you were paying for it, and not the company."

He sipped his scotch and soda. "That's because I didn't want to explain to our accountant that I'd torn your other dress while seducing you. But no matter how it was paid for, that dress was a good business decision. When you run the company the lines get blurred, anyway." He eyed her over the rim of his glass.

"So I'm learning."

Paul came to the table. "About ready to knock 'em dead again, Kerry?"

She laughed. "Some of them came in that way. I'd be satisfied if we can put a little life in them."

Paul squeezed her shoulder. "Those new numbers we rehearsed should do the trick."

They should have, Kerry thought as they worked their way through to the last number, but the crowd still didn't really catch fire. Again, her expectations were probably askew.

"Good set," Judd said as he handed her into the limo. "Tomorrow night we'll see how they react at the Besotted Fox."

"I hope the Besotted Fox gets a more enthusiastic clientele. I just didn't feel any chemistry here, Judd."

He shrugged. "That happens, which is why I booked you into two different clubs for your time here."

She gazed at him as rainbows of neon slid over him. She wanted to follow the path of the light with her fingers, but if she did they wouldn't talk, and she needed some answers. "If this were the only club you'd tested me in, would I get a contract on the basis of these performances?"

He hesitated and at last met her gaze. "No."

Her stomach clenched. So her expectations hadn't been too high. She hadn't electrified the audiences at Compulsions, or the anonymous company representatives who had wandered in, and that was what Judd had been looking for. "What if the same thing happens at the Besotted Fox?" Her heart pounded rapidly as she awaited his answer.

Instead of replying, he took her hands and turned them over to kiss her palms.

"You'd send me home with no contract, wouldn't you?"

He glanced up, his eyes luminous. "I don't know what I'd do."

Her fingers curled into fists. "Yes, you do. You haven't come this far in the music business by making decisions based on sentiment."

He rubbed his thumbs across her knuckles. "I've come this far without meeting someone like you."

His statement stunned her. Would he keep her on, despite her inability to command an audience, because he wanted her? She imagined the smirks and company gossip, the barely suppressed disdain as he tried to make her into a star because it suited his own needs to keep her there.

She swallowed. "Then if you don't know what you'd do, I'll tell you my plan. If the crowd at the Besotted Fox doesn't like me any better than the bunch at Compulsions, I'm going home, whether you send me or not. I won't be the boss's misguided project, the untalented little hussy who's trying to sleep her way to fame and fortune."

The muscles in his face tightened. "Do you think my judgment about you is screwed up because we're lovers?"

"I sincerely hope not. I need the unvarnished truth from you, Judd, and I want to be treated the way you would treat anyone who came to town to audition for you."

"Too late for that."

"I meant—"

"I know what you meant." He took her by the shoulders and pulled her toward him. "And I won't shine you on, Kerry."

She gazed up at him as he lowered his head. "Promise?"

"Scout's honor," he murmured, just before he kissed her.

As he reached beneath her chiffon skirt, she pinned his hand between her thighs and disengaged her lips from his. "Stop."

His hand moved farther up. "Don't want to."

"What about Zorba?"

"Besides paying him extra to chauffeur us late at night, I've also paid him to keep his eyes straight ahead."

"And the other cars?"

"I'll be discreet. People drive too fast in Manhattan to figure out subtleties going on in somebody else's car. I've been the soul of propriety all night while you enticed me in that dress. Kiss me, Kerry, and let me be a rascal for a while."

With a sigh of delight she parted her thighs, and the rascal pleasured her with deft fingers until she would have cried out had he not muffled her response with a deep kiss.

When she stilled, he lifted his head and smiled gently. "I love that about women. You can have your private little fireworks and practically nothing shows. We could drive around all night and I could keep giving you orgasm after orgasm, and the world wouldn't know." His eyes twinkled. "Want to?"

She took a steadying breath. "I believe in mutual satisfaction."

"Which is my good fortune, because we're almost home. Although in my condition it would be nice if someone could airlift me into the bedroom."

Kerry grinned and touched the bulge in his slacks.

"Don't," he warned.

Taking pity on him, she removed her hand.

"We'll just sit here a moment," he said with a heartfelt sigh. "As I said, women have all the luck."

"And men have all the monuments," Kerry added with a chuckle. "Many of them dedicated to that certain male idiosyncrasy."

"I don't know about that."

"Consider the Washington Monument, the Eiffel Tower, the Leaning Tower of Pisa, the Seattle Space Needle, even New York skyscrapers. Why, the Empire State Building is a clear representation of—"

His voice rumbled low. "Could we discuss something else?"

"How about the concert you're going to give me in about ten minutes on the saxophone?"

"That'll work. Hey, I think I'm ready to walk already. Only I'm not giving you a concert," he said as he opened the limo door.

"Please, Judd."

He helped her out. "Ask me something else and your wish is my command."

"This is what I want."

He waved to Zorba and took her elbow as they walked into the lobby. "Why?"

"This will sound really corny."

"So will that saxophone. Trust me, Kerry, you don't want this." He ushered them into the elevator and pushed the button for his floor.

She watched his supple fingers. She'd been drawn to the image of him playing from the beginning of their relationship. "I think the saxophone has a lot to do with who you are. I think I'll know you better after I hear you play."

"Yeah." He chuckled ruefully. "You'll know I can't play the sax worth a damn, that's what you'll know."

"I don't care how well you play."

"Sure. You're a top-rate musician who's studied all her life, and you don't care how I play? Tell me another story."

She walked past him into the apartment. The saxophone case still rested on the coffee table where she'd first found it. She turned to him. "Play for me," she coaxed.

He tossed the keys in his hand. "Maybe someday."

"Now. We're out of balance, Judd. I'm always the vulnerable one, up on stage and in the studio. You're always in charge."

"I wasn't particularly in charge back in the limo."

"Well, that's different." But she'd use that vulnerability if she had to. She unlatched the case and took out the gold-toned instrument. She rubbed her fingers up and down the bell and glanced at him. He'd stopped tossing his keys.

"I *really* want you to play this for me," she said, dropping her voice a register. One strap of her dress had slipped over her shoulder. She let it stay that way as she gave him a smoldering look. "A saxophone gets me hot."

"Kerry—"

"I can tell by the way you kiss that you haven't forgotten how to play. You can make this sax moan, just like you can make me moan."

He swallowed, and his tawny eyes became the color of liquid gold.

"I'll even get it ready, and when you're finished, I'll be ready...for anything." In school she'd tried about every instrument that existed, so she knew her way around this one. She attached the mouthpiece and picked up a reed. "Want me to suck on your reed?"

He made a strangled sound in his throat and stepped forward, reaching for her.

She backed away, moistening the reed as she held his gaze. Then she attached the reed to the mouthpiece. "Play first. Then I'm yours."

He moved as if hypnotized and took the instrument from her hand. Her gaze never leaving his, she sank slowly onto the sofa. He put the strap over his head, and as she'd expected, a subtle transformation took place. His fingers found the keys automatically and his body relaxed to accommodate the heft of the instrument.

As he lipped the mouthpiece, he gave her a look that caused the equivalent of a nuclear meltdown. He'd accepted the challenge and he would seduce her with his song.

A shiver ran through her as the first notes, sultry as the humid New York night, filled the apartment. He improvised, spilling a jazz melody over her like warm caramel, surrounding her with lazy, sensuous notes that melted together into pictures of long nights, twisted sheets and slippery bodies. His fingers caressed the keys with the same loving precision they'd lavished on her. She ached for him.

Through half-closed eyes he watched her as he played. That heavy-lidded gaze drew her as no other expression of his had. She reveled in the languid sweetness of it, the whisper of sin, the hint of decadence. After this, he could do as he pleased with her. She was his fool.

The sax wailed to a climax, and for a moment, he closed his eyes and lived the music. She'd known he would, had sensed the depths in him that the music would touch when he created it himself. And when he created it for her. She needed no other declaration.

Words were nothing compared to this outpouring from his soul.

The last notes drifted between them, and he opened his eyes.

She held out her arms.

Watching her, he lifted the strap over his head and laid the instrument carefully on a chair before walking to her. Then he took her outstretched arms and pulled her to her feet. "Is that what you wanted?"

"Yes."

"It's all I have."

"And all I want."

His kiss was rich with feeling. He undressed her slowly for the first time, as if there was no hurry, as if they had a lifetime. Kerry believed they did.

His slow, deliberate loving carried more meaning than any of the frenzied couplings they'd enjoyed in the few days they'd been together. She undressed him with the same care and reverence.

He lowered her to the couch, started to enter her, then drew back with a soft exclamation.

"What?" She cupped his face in both hands. "What, my darling?"

He searched her face. "You know what. Would you have stopped me?"

Her heart wrenched. Would she have stopped him from loving her without protection? Slowly she shook her head.

His voice was gentle. "Then you're a fool."

So she was. His fool.

He reached back for his slacks, found the packet and put on the condom with swift, impatient motions.

Kerry wanted to cry. The hard-won communion of souls was gone. When he came to her, his first thrust was fierce. A tear trickled from the corner of her eye.

Dismay filled his eyes. "Did I hurt you?"

She shook her head and grasped his hips. Tears clogged her throat. "I loved your song," she choked out.

"Ah, Kerry." He kissed her softly and began to move inside her. His loving was wonderful, but she couldn't forget the tenderness with which he'd almost taken her, before he'd refocused on reality. As his knowing rhythm brought her to a searing climax, she cried out for what was . . . and for what might have been.

"COME WITH ME to Central Park this afternoon." Kerry adjusted a pearl necklace at her throat as she made a last inspection of her appearance in the bathroom mirror the next morning.

"Can't spare the time." Judd cinched a tie up under his collar.

She met his gaze in the mirror. "How do you exist being constantly indoors? You even run on an indoor track."

"I'm used to staying inside, I guess. But I worry about Rachel sometimes. Kids need fresh air. That's why we live here, across from the park. When she was younger I had a nanny who would take her there a lot. Now she's getting a little old for that, but not old enough to go by herself."

"And you don't go with her?"

He sighed and glanced down, adjusting cuffs that didn't need it. "The business gets more demanding every day."

Before he'd lowered his gaze, she'd glimpsed the conflict in his eyes. It couldn't be easy juggling the demands of his job with the obligations of a single father. He needed help, either on the job or with Rachel, but he wasn't the sort of man to ask for help. "I understand," she said gently, touching his arm.

He shot her a look of such yearning that she was taken aback. Then the buzzer rang, indicating Zorba had arrived to take him to the office, and he quickly composed his expression. "See you tonight," he said, giving her a quick, fierce kiss before he left the room.

She stared after him, remembering how he'd serenaded her on the saxophone the night before and how relaxed and sure he'd been for a little while afterward, as he'd loved her. For that brief time he'd seemed to be living fully, instead of carefully weighing the consequences of his behavior.

As she put the finishing touches on her makeup, she thought about the glimpses she'd caught of Judd's unrestrained nature. The first was finding him on her porch with his socks off. Then he'd taken the risk of making love to her, even going so far as to march fully clothed into the shower. Then last night in the limo he'd secretly loved her, and then immersed himself in playing the sax for her.

She brought out that side of him apparently. But what happened when she wasn't around? It seemed obvious that he usually denied his unbridled instincts, instincts that were a true expression of his soul.

The buzzer sounded again. Zorba had deposited Judd at the studio in record time as usual, and he was back to pick her up. The pace of life here made Kerry's head ache. She and Judd had decided arriving together each morning would only feed the rumor mill, so Zorba made two trips as if he was picking Kerry up at her hotel.

She hurried downstairs and out into the steam-iron morning. Zorba held the door of the limo for her.

"Can I ride up front with you this time?" she asked.

He looked surprised, but he closed the back door and opened the front passenger door. "If you want."

As they pulled away from the curb, she turned and studied his strong Greek profile and steel gray hair. "I appreciate how discreet you've been about this arrangement between Judd and me."

"You're welcome."

She smiled at the courtly way he acknowledged her gratitude. "Judd really trusts you, Zorba."

He nodded.

She could tell he wouldn't offer information, so she took a more aggressive approach. "How long have you known him?"

"Twelve years."

"You've been driving for him that long?"

Zorba shook his head. "I had a little boat dock on the coast of Maine. Taught Judd and Steve how to sail. Sold Steve his first boat."

"Then you were around when..." She couldn't bring herself to complete the sentence.

"Yes."

"Tell me what happened, Zorba. I need to know."

He slowed the limo. "Steve was the wild one of the two. Judd had his moments, but Steve loved to test the limits. I told him not to take the boat out that day, but he called me an old woman. I led the search party, and I...found them."

Kerry shuddered. "Judd was part of the search party."

"He was like a crazy person. I thought he'd kill himself trying to find them, until I reminded him about Rachel. Then he pulled back."

And he's still pulling back, Kerry thought.

"Not long after, I sold the dock, the rental boats, everything. I just didn't enjoy the business anymore. Judd offered me a job, and I took it."

Kerry took a deep, quivering breath. "Thank you for telling me."

"And now let me ask you something. Do you care about him?"

"Yes. Very much."

"I think he needs someone, someone to make him laugh and be a little crazy again. To take risks. Not the kind of risk his brother took with the boat. Emotional risks."

"I think we're both doing some of that emotional risk taking right now."

"But I thought you wanted to be a star."

"I do."

He stared out the windshield. "When that happens, if it happens, what then?"

"I—I don't know." She realized they were sitting at the curb outside the building housing Lighthouse Records, had been sitting there for some time. "We're both in the entertainment business, so I suppose we can just—"

"Don't forget he has a daughter."

"What are you saying?"

Zorba gazed at her, his dark eyes intense. "I'm saying that she figures into everything. Don't expect him to be your jet-setting lover, because he can't be that. He's told me he's avoided getting involved with recording stars for just that reason. Why he's made an exception with you, I have no idea."

Kerry returned his gaze as the puzzle he'd posed slowly settled over her. Then she blanched when the only possible answer flashed through her mind as if etched by a laser beam. *He's made an exception because he doesn't think I'll make it.*

13

CENTRAL PARK LAY like a giant cake frosted in green surrounded by a protective ring of granite skyscrapers. The dense foliage cushioned the noise of traffic. The laughter of children and the clip-clop of a horse pulling a carriage brought a smile to Kerry's face as she wandered along a path. People *did* stroll in Central Park, as if they'd checked their ambitions and worries at some imaginary gate before stepping onto the welcoming grass.

She had no map, and the park covered far more acres than she'd at first imagined, but instinct guided her to a small lake. The sight of a body of water, even if there were no tides, foghorns or gulls, calmed her. She'd heard that somewhere in the park rowboats could be rented. One day she'd try that, although a rowboat on a lake wouldn't take the place of sailing the *Leprechaun II*.

She'd stuffed a stale crust from the bread box in Judd's kitchen into her skirt pocket, just in case she encountered ducks or pigeons. As she walked to the water's edge, a flotilla of mallards in a V-formation arrowed through the water toward her. Breaking the bread into small chunks, she tossed it out. The ducks broke formation and paddled after the food, the green necks of the males iridescent in the sunlight as they dived for pieces of bread.

As Kerry fed the ducks, the tension eased from between her shoulder blades. If she lived in New York, she'd come here every morning to feed the ducks, just as she'd gone on the beach every morning in Eternity. But perhaps she wouldn't live in New York. Perhaps her talent just wasn't good enough.

Judd's belief in her coupled with her own determination had carried her this far. But Zorba had a legitimate point, and he spoke from years of experience with Judd. In his own gruff way, Zorba had been warning her, and with apparent good reason. If Judd had declared recording stars off-limits because of his obligation to his daughter, why had he made an exception in Kerry's case?

She dusted bread crumbs from her hands. Maybe Judd couldn't help himself. Without Rachel in New York, he'd allowed passion to overrule good sense. But Rachel would come back. Perhaps Judd's awareness of that had kept him from making any personal commitment to her.

For he hadn't, of course. Kerry meandered beside the lake as she replayed all her encounters with Judd. They'd enjoyed each other with gusto, but there'd been no pillow talk about a future together, no declarations of love.

Any way Kerry looked at the situation, their glorious affair seemed doomed. If she became a success, Judd would drop her the minute Rachel returned. If she failed—even if that prompted a commitment from Judd—she couldn't imagine remaining with him. She'd be reminded every day that he moved in a world she didn't have the talent to enter.

They had to talk. Perhaps he wouldn't care to answer the questions she'd ask him, but even his silence would tell her what she needed to know. Her mother used to say, "If you don't want to see the dirt, don't lift up the rug." But her mother never allowed dirt to collect under rugs, and she'd raised her six children the same way. Tonight Kerry would talk to Judd.

She'd reached the far end of the lake by the time she came to that conclusion. Perspiration dampened her blouse, and she lifted her hair away from the nape of her neck. But she didn't mind the heat so much here, where she could enjoy the dappled shadows of trees and the sparkle of sun on the water.

She couldn't imagine why all New Yorkers didn't visit the park at least once a day for a walk or a picnic. Except they, like Judd, were too busy. She wondered if she'd ever become too busy. Or too famous. She'd read the complaints of stars who said they weren't free to live a normal life, and she'd laughed. Who would want a normal life when you could have fame? But if she couldn't even walk through a park like this, if . . .

She paused and listened. Somewhere nearby a woman was singing. Kerry caught the last line, "Safe in your arms forevermore," and the woman's song ended. Kerry's skin prickled, as if a soft breeze had touched it, yet the air was still.

A child giggled and applauded. "'Gain, Bevin!"

Bevin obliged.

Kerry had left the path and moved toward the song almost before she realized what she was doing. She knew that song. Or at least she thought she did. She couldn't think where she'd heard it, but somehow the melody reminded her of Eternity. Maybe her mother had sung it long ago. Yet the words weren't familiar.

Her low heels sank into the soft grass as she climbed a small rise. On the other side, in the shade of a towering elm, a young woman sat on a red-checkered tablecloth with a towheaded girl of about four sprawled on her stomach, her chin propped on her hands as she listened, her gaze fastened on the young woman's face.

The woman was dressed in a blue cotton skirt and white sleeveless blouse, her brown hair pulled up into a ponytail on the left side of her head. Her voice was untrained, but clear and sweet. The melody taunted Kerry with a memory she couldn't place. But as she listened, she could smell the salt air of Eternity and hear the splash of waves on the sand.

"Tides that call me, sails that swell," the young woman sang, "and I must rove, to love you well."

The little girl caught sight of Kerry and started to say something. Kerry put a finger to her lips, but it was too late. The young woman had noticed the child's change in expression and stopped singing. She turned and glanced uncertainly at Kerry.

"I'm sorry to disturb you." Kerry walked down the hillside toward the pair. "But that song seems so familiar to me. What is it?"

"It's called 'The Beacon,'" the woman replied in a faint brogue. "My grandmother used to sing it in Gaelic, but Tiffany doesn't understand that, so I'm teaching her the English translation."

Tiffany had scrambled to her feet as they talked. "My Bevin sings real good," she announced. She had a smear of grape jelly on her cheek.

"Yes, she does," Kerry agreed. She opened her purse and rummaged for a piece of paper. All she found was a napkin left over from the deli sandwich she'd ordered for lunch. "Could you tell me the words, please, Bevin? And teach me the tune?"

Bevin glanced at her watch. "I have to be getting Tiffany back soon. Her mother wants her dressed for dinner by half-past four, because they'll be going out."

"I'm a fast learner," Kerry said, unsure why she had such a desperate need to capture this song. It was old-fashioned, a folk tune of unknown origin—not at all the sort of thing she usually sang. Yet she wanted to feel the shape of the words in her mouth, the melody rising from her throat. Maybe it was nothing more than homesickness, because the song evoked Eternity so strongly for her.

"I'll tell you while Tiffany and I fold up the tablecloth and get ready," Bevin said. "I can't be late. Once before I kept Tiffany in the park overtime, and her mother nearly let me go."

"I *never* want Bevin to go," Tiffany declared, her hands on her hips.

"Then just sing the song slowly," Kerry said, "and I'll write the words down. I can probably remember the tune."

Bevin cleared her throat and began singing as she moved the cooler and picked up a corner of the tablecloth. "You've set me free, to find my way..."

Kerry held the napkin against the side of her purse and scribbled furiously without looking up. Once or twice she anticipated the next line and was right. *Had* she heard this before?

Bevin finished the song and picked up the cooler with the tablecloth folded on top. "Got it?"

Kerry hurried through the last sentence of the final verse. "I think so."

"I have time for you to sing it back to me, if you want."

"Okay." Holding the napkin, Kerry began. The key was perfect for her. She grew more confident as she finished the first verse and, when she came to the refrain, found herself projecting as if to reach across the footlights.

"Shine for me through tempest's wrath, shine for me through blackest night," she sang, her voice rising with the swelling melody. "Show to me the guilded path, and I'll return, beloved light." A lighthouse. Of course she'd be drawn to it, she thought.

Her heart beating faster, she sang the second verse, and the third. By the time she came to the refrain for the last time, she owned the song—or it owned her. Such a communion with a piece of music had never happened to her before. The power of it left her shaken as the sound of the last note sailed upward into the trees.

Bevin had set down the cooler, and when Kerry finished, she began to clap. Tiffany did, too, jumping up and down as she smacked her pudgy fingers together. The applause seemed to echo, because Kerry heard the sound of clapping from behind her, too. She turned and found a dozen people gathered—men in business suits, women pushing strollers, an old woman with a toothless smile, a kid standing on a skateboard. They clapped and clapped, while Kerry stood in amazed silence. The expression on their faces was what she'd missed all those nights at Compulsions when she'd stared into the bored, uninterested eyes of the nightclub patrons.

"Thank you," she managed to say.

"What's your name?" the boy with the skateboard called out.

"Kerry Muldoon," she replied.

"You sing for a living?" he persisted.

"Yes, I do." She realized now was the time to put in a plug for herself. "I'll be appearing at the Besotted Fox for the next two nights."

"Are you going to sing that song?" a man with a *Wall Street Journal* under one arm asked.

"I . . ." She couldn't imagine it would fit. The band wouldn't know it, so she'd have to sing a cappella. "Yes, I am," she said.

"Then we'll be there," the man said. "My wife would love that song."

Kerry gazed after the man as he walked away. Then the others began to leave, a few offering comments about how nice she'd sounded. *My wife would love that song.* There it was. Up until now, people in New York had liked what she'd offered them, but she doubted they'd loved it. The response from the crowd at the reception didn't really count. They wouldn't have had the bad manners to ignore her. But these people in the park had loved her song. She'd seen it in their expressions.

Tucking the napkin into her purse and thanking the young woman, she hurried back to Judd's apartment. She had some practicing to do before tonight's performance.

JUDD SAT in the back of the Besotted Fox sipping ale. With pictures of scarlet-coated riders on the dark-paneled walls and hunting trophies flanking the shining mahogany bar, the Besotted Fox probably looked more like an English pub than anything in London, he mused with a smile.

His smile faded as he considered how the crowd was reacting to Kerry. They'd given her polite applause, but nobody seemed impressed. If she could ignite this crowd, he'd send her on the road in September as the opening act for Saucy Sisters, one of Lighthouse's top groups, which was going on tour this fall.

She would leave about the time Rachel came back to school, and by the time Kerry returned from tour, Judd would expect her to be well on her way to fame and fortune. Except it didn't look as if she'd be going out on tour. And he'd have to be the one to tell her.

He wondered if she'd keep trying or give up. Either way she wouldn't want to have much to do with him. The Greeks used to kill the bearer of bad news. The hell of it was he wasn't sure what was wrong with her act. She sang like an angel and managed to look both sexy and wholesome at the same time. But she hadn't captured the imagination of the audiences, and even Henry Gridley, who liked Kerry personally, had dropped hints that she should be dumped. Judd had always figured he'd lose her, but he didn't want it to be this way.

She'd come to the last song of the set, and he prepared himself to be encouraging but noncommittal when she came over to get his reaction. Of course she knew it wasn't working. She'd figured that out at Compulsions, and she also knew he wouldn't sign her on the basis of their personal relationship. As she'd said, she wouldn't want that, and neither would he. He respected her too much for that.

Instead of launching into the Phil Collins number she'd traditionally used to close the set, Kerry walked over to Paul and had a brief conference with him. Judd's throat constricted. Would she quit now, in the middle of a booking? He didn't think she operated that way, but her nerves might be shot now that her last chance seemed to be slipping through her fingers. He wondered if the manager of the Besotted Fox would settle for some excellent dance music from the band as a substitute for Kerry. Damn, this was a miserable situation.

He waited, jaw clenched, to see what she would do. Paul replaced his guitar in its stand. Not a good sign. Kerry approached the mike and he gripped the handle of his ale mug.

"I'd like to end this set with a number a little out of the ordinary," Kerry said, and laughed. "The band doesn't know it, so I'll sing it unaccompanied."

Judd half rose from his seat. What the hell—? She was throwing in an unrehearsed number?

"I'd like to dedicate this song to the wife of a man who reads the *Wall Street Journal* and took a walk in Central Park today."

Judd stared at her. This was the craziest thing he'd ever heard. Maybe she'd finally cracked under the tension. Except she looked cool as a cucumber—more poised, in fact, than she'd seemed all evening.

Her eyes drifted shut and her fingers closed around the microphone stand. "You've set me free, to find my way," she began in the magic voice that had entranced him that first morning on the beach, "Although your silence begs me stay."

A chill skittered down his spine. The melody was exquisite, but the lyrics . . . He listened, an unwilling captive of those words.

"And I must go, despite the pain. If Fate is kind, we'll meet again."

The audience fell silent as their attention focused on the woman in black standing in the spotlight, her body swaying as she moved into the song's refrain. Oh, God. This was it. The joy of seeing her master the audience was nearly as great as his agony. This was the moment he'd lose her.

She sang as if looking deep into his heart. "For there are truths that I must learn, roads that take a different turn."

His throat closed. She was so beautiful, with the spotlight sparkling over her raven hair and creamy shoulders. This was what he'd wanted; this was the path he'd have chosen for her. Somehow she'd found it herself. This song, and perhaps others like it, would bring her the fame she sought.

"But when my soul has drunk its fill, when the tide has lost its pull," she sang, her gaze finding him, "then, my love, I'll turn for shore, safe in your arms, forever-more."

Hope shone through his despair for one brief moment. But no, it was only a song. In the real world, once she'd left she'd never return. He'd read once that fame was like drinking seawater—it made you thirsty for more.

When she finished, there was the tiny moment of silence that shouts success louder than thunderous applause. Then the ovation came crashing in. People whistled and pounded on tables. At last. Judd closed his eyes and wondered how he'd make it through the next few days, knowing that his separation from Kerry had begun.

KERRY HURRIED BACK to Judd's table, her heart fluttering wildly. "Well?"

He gave her a slow smile, although his eyes ... Why did he look so sad? "You don't need me to tell you," he said. "Where did you get that number?"

Her enthusiasm returned. "It was the most amazing thing. I found a nanny in the park today who was singing it to a little kid. She taught it to me."

He nodded. "It's obviously what you should be singing. Did you get the nanny's name?"

"Bevin is all I know, and the little girl she's caring for is Tiffany. Does it matter?"

"Only if she knows more songs like this, but don't worry about it. We'll find others with a similar appeal for you to work into a set. You're a natural with that kind of music."

"They liked me." Kerry had thought she might fly apart from the excitement of the audience's response.

"They loved you," Judd corrected.

"Yes." And did he? The world had shifted in the past few minutes, and she needed to know what he was thinking. But when she noticed Paul had just grabbed a chair to sit with them, she knew now wasn't the time.

"So, Kerry, what's the name of that song, anyway?" Paul asked.

"It's called 'The Beacon.'"

He put his arm around her shoulders and gave her a quick hug. "I think it's called money in the bank. And what better company to make that song number one on the charts than Lighthouse? Some things are just meant to be."

"I guess you're right," Kerry said. She kept glancing at Judd. He looked proud of her, very proud. But there was some other emotion hovering in the background, shading his eyes. It looked a lot like pain.

14

KERRY FELT the change in Judd from the moment they stepped into the limo. His kiss was restrained, his touch undemanding. The crazy, mindless passion they'd enjoyed had evaporated. His CEO persona was firmly in place.

Struggling to get her bearings, she responded automatically as they discussed whether adding any accompaniment would ruin her new song, or whether soft backup vocals would be a good idea. But the fire had left his gaze, as if he'd deliberately doused it. She had no doubt he'd offer her a contract now. And when she signed it, she could be signing away any hope of a relationship with Judd Roarke. What if she'd known that from the beginning? Would she have changed anything?

They entered the apartment and she walked over to the sofa and sat down. Judd's saxophone still rested in its case on the coffee table. She wondered if he'd play it after they parted. A sob threatened to erupt and she looked away from the saxophone case.

"Would you like a drink?" Judd asked. "I think there's some champagne in the—"

She glanced up. "I'd like to talk."

He tossed his jacket aside and walked toward her. "All right." He chose to sit in a wing chair opposite her, instead of beside her. She wasn't surprised. "Go ahead," he said carefully.

She laced her fingers together and stared down at her hands. Now that the moment was here she wasn't certain how to begin. She didn't want to reveal that Zorba had clued her in. The chauffeur might get in trouble for something she should probably thank him for.

She swallowed and looked at Judd. "Until this moment neither of us knew for certain what my future would be."

"That's true." His voice was measured and even.

She wanted to scream at him not to tighten up on her, but what else could she expect? She'd succeeded, so now he had to pull away. "After tonight, it looks as if I might have a career with Lighthouse, after all."

"No doubt about it. Musical tastes are always recycling, and there seems to be a movement back to the folk music of the seventies. Henry will probably turn you into a nineties version of Joan Baez."

Kerry flinched. She didn't want to be a version of someone else, and she also hated the way Judd had begun talking about her as a commodity. This was supposed to be her moment of triumph, but it was overridden by her fear that she was losing him.

She approached the subject obliquely. "Once you said our personal relationship had probably compromised our business arrangement. Is that still the way you view it?"

"Judging from where we are now, apparently it hasn't compromised it. You're on your way."

You've set me free, to find my way. Her dry throat ached from the pressure of tears she must not shed. "Has our business arrangement compromised our personal relationship?"

He was silent for a moment. Then he took a long, shuddering breath. "Yes."

His answer knifed through her. "Why?"

"You don't realize it yet, but your life has changed forever. You're destined for stardom, Kerry, and all that it means."

"Tell me what it means, Judd." She fought rising hysteria. "Because I always thought it would mean wonderful things, and I don't feel wonderful right now."

His expression softened. "You will," he said gently. "In a couple of months I'll have faded to the status of a good friend, somebody who helped you on the way up. You'll be way beyond this interlude. You'll see it for what it was, a time you needed support. And I was able to offer—"

"Stop!" She leapt to her feet, her voice shaking. "Is that all this has been to you? Giving the proper encouragement to a potential star? If so, you can shove your precious contract right up your—"

"Don't be an idiot." He rose to face her. "I made love to you because I wanted to. If it helped you over a rough time, so much the better. But believe me, I had plenty of selfish reasons, too."

"Then why does all that have to change?"

His smile was sad. "Because it always does. You're on a rocket now. I can't expect you to remember some paltry earthbound pleasures we had."

"That is the stupidest reasoning I've ever heard." She felt a moment of wild hope. Had he pulled back because he thought that in the flush of success she'd leave him? That was a problem she could fix. "How dare you measure the level of my commitment to you? How dare you assume I'll toss this relationship aside once I've hit the big time?"

"I assume, because I've spent years in the business, and I've watched it happen countless times."

She felt she was getting close to something. "Has it ever happened to you?"

He hesitated. "Once."

"So now you're going to tell me you once had a love affair with someone like Bonnie Raitt and she dumped you? Who's the glowing comet on the recording scene who threw over Judd Roarke to pursue fame and fortune?" She saw the words plow through his composure, but she didn't care. His composure be damned.

He shook his head, glanced away. "She's dead."

The words hit her like a blow to the stomach. She gasped.

"It's okay." He gave her a bleak look. "It happened years ago."

Her voice was a whisper. "I'm sorry. I didn't mean to . . ."

"But you're right. She's part of the reason I expect you to take off. She found a love affair to be too much trouble—which it is, Kerry. Face facts. You aren't going to have time for hearts and flowers. You're a performer now."

"And you're pulling away out of self-defense?"

He regarded her silently.

She wanted to think that was all of it, but the explanation didn't fit his personality. She had to keep lifting the damned rug. "I don't buy it. Tell me what the real problem is."

His gaze was tortured. "Rachel."

So Zorba was right. Her stomach churned. "Could you . . . explain that?"

He walked over to the window that looked out on the shadowed trees of the park and shoved his hands in his pockets. "She deserves whatever spare time I have, which isn't much. If you and I kept our relationship going, I'd fly to the city where you're performing just to snatch moments alone with you. I'd plan my weeks so I'd be free when you came back to New York. And in my frenzy to be with you, I could end up shoving Rachel to the back of my life."

"Include Rachel! She seems to like me. The three of us could—"

"No. I won't drag her around like that."

Kerry's shoulders sagged. He was right, of course. Children needed the security of a routine, not a frenetic life on the road. She wouldn't expect Judd to ask Rachel to live for his—or her—convenience.

Her throat hurt so much she wondered if she'd ever sing again. "I guess there's nothing more to say. Perhaps it would be best if I moved back to the Salisbury."

"Maybe it would." He sounded exhausted.

"We never had a single hope of something lasting, did we, Judd?"

He shook his head, and when he spoke, his voice was heavy with remorse. "I suppose you wonder why, if I knew that, I made love to you."

"No, I don't."

He turned, obviously surprised. "Why not?"

"Because I know why we made love. We're perfect for each other."

With a strangled noise deep in his throat, he crossed the room and pulled her into his arms. She held on for dear life, and the tears came.

He kissed her wet face, her quivering mouth, her convulsing throat. Then he carried her, still crying, into the bedroom. His image blurred in the wake of tears she couldn't stop as she made love to him for the last time.

KERRY MOVED zombielike through the packing pro-
cess. Judd was out running in Central Park. She
planned to be gone from the apartment before he came
back. Their lovemaking the night before was the only
goodbye she cared to have. They'd said all that had to
be said.

First thing this morning Judd had called the studio
and arranged for Kerry to begin work recording the new
song. They'd continue the work on Sunday, if necessary, and she'd go back to Eternity Monday morning.
Then he'd told Kerry he'd decided to drive up and see
Rachel for the weekend. Kerry was relieved. She'd have
a hard time concentrating on her work knowing he was
somewhere in the Lighthouse offices where she might
accidentally run into him at any moment.

She'd zipped her black dress into the garment bag just
as the buzzer sounded announcing Zorba's arrival. She
didn't take any last looks as she hefted the bag and left
the apartment.

RACHEL TORE DOWN the porch steps as Judd pulled into
the driveway. "Daddy, come and see my room!"

Her laughter, her energy, her skinny little arms
around his neck, her bubble-gum breath—he soaked
up everything that was Rachel. Her presence flowed
over his bruised heart, easing the pain. He would keep
her in New York with him. Why had he ever imagined
he could let her stay in Massachusetts with her grandparents? He and Rachel needed each other, belonged
together.

"What about your room?" he asked as she hung on
his arm, nearly pulling him off-balance as they climbed
the porch steps.

Stella held the screen door open for them. "She was so excited to show you. We just finished putting up the curtains about an hour ago."

"Been redecorating, huh?" he said to Rachel.

"Daddy, it is way cool. I picked everything myself. Grandma let me help sew the curtains, and on Monday we're getting a portable CD player to go on the shelves we painted." She swung his hand as they walked up the stairs to the second floor. "I've already got one CD, *janet.*"

"Janet Jackson?"

"Yep. I know she's not with Lighthouse, but the songs are just way cool, Dad."

Judd glanced down at his bouncing daughter. She'd grown up around all kinds of music, but she'd never been particularly interested in rock before. Now she was murmuring something rhythmically under her breath as they climbed the rest of the stairs. It sounded to Judd like rap.

At the landing she released his hand and raced ahead into her room. "Come see! Come see!"

He walked in with a tolerant smile on his face, expecting pastels and flowers. His smile faded as he gazed at a color scheme that punched him in the eye with vivid shapes and colors. The curtains were a psychedelic mix of red and purple that made him think of bruises in various stages of healing. In each corner of the room sat a beanbag chair, one red and one purple. The red quilt on the bed glowed like a stoplight, and the startling effect was heightened with purple throw pillows shaped in triangles, hearts and circles.

He vaguely remembered that watercolors of kittens and puppies had once hung on the walls. Now Christian Slater grinned down at him from one poster and Jason Priestly from another.

"Isn't it great?" Rachel asked.

"Great," Judd replied, still adjusting. "Sure is bright."

"Yup. I got tired of that baby stuff that was in here. Grandma said we could change it, and I could choose the colors. Dad, do you think, when I turn ten next month, I could get my ears pierced?"

He stared at her.

"Just one hole in each ear," she said quickly. "I wouldn't want two holes yet. Maybe later. One's fine, really."

"Uh, we'll see." He shot a glance behind him, where Stella lingered in the hallway. "What do you think, Stella?"

"Ten's probably a good age, if she promises to be careful about daubing her ears with alcohol."

Judd frowned. Pierced ears. Another thing he didn't have a clue about.

The phone rang, and Rachel lurched around him and ran out the door. "That's probably Marcie. Excuse me," she hollered over her shoulder as she bounded down the stairs.

"We have a red phone on order," Stella explained, walking into the room. "She insisted we not leave that pink one she had in here before, so that's why she has to go rushing downstairs when the phone rings. And it usually is for her. The kids have formed a regular little social group, and they call each other constantly."

Judd turned his back on Christian Slater. "Doesn't that drive you nuts?"

Stella laughed. "The phone or the poster?"

"Both."

"Actually, all this brings back fond memories."

Judd shook his head. "I've only been gone a couple of weeks, and she already seems so much older."

She gave him a level gaze. "Kids grow up fast."

"Grandma, can I go to the beach with Marcie and her mom?" Rachel called up the stairs.

Judd glanced at Stella. "Marcie and her mother don't have a boat, do they?"

Stella's eyes softened with compassion. "No. I'd never let Rachel out on a boat, Judd. You know that. But maybe I should ask Rachel to stay home, anyhow. After all, you just got here, and we could all—"

"No. Let her go." He managed a smile. "I could use some time in the hammock out back, anyway."

"Okay, Kerry," Tom said gently over the intercom. "Try that first line again."

Kerry took a deep breath and blew it out slowly. She was keeping everyone here from their usual Sunday activities, but she had no power to send them home. Judd had left word they were to get a decent version of "The Beacon" on tape this weekend. With no windows in the studio and no clocks, she'd lost track of time. And she'd begun to hate the song.

She especially hated this latest version, but Tom seemed in love with it, and the band was having a ball with the new rhythms. She waited through the intro and started the song again. "You've se-et me free-ee, to fi-ind my wa-ay." And so had Judd. She was free, all right. Without Judd, the road to fame stretched ahead of her like a boulder-strewn path leading to a glacier-topped mountain peak.

"You came in a beat too soon," Tom said.

"I'm sorry." Kerry rubbed her temples. "I'm sure everyone's as sick of this as I am."

"Maybe we need a break," Tom suggested. "And some food. I'll call the deli."

The thought of food made Kerry's stomach heave. "You guys go ahead and eat. I'll just have coffee."

Paul stood and stretched his arms over his head. "Let's all walk down there, get some of the stink blown off us. Come on, Kerry. The fresh air'll do you good."

Joe laughed. "What Paul is saying is that we'll come back high on carbon-monoxide fumes and we'll play better."

"Thanks for the offer." Kerry forced a smile. "I'd rather stay here and go over the song a few times by myself."

"Listen to Uncle Paulie," Paul warned, wagging a finger at her. "You'll get stale. Come with us. Maybe we'll have a beer."

"No, thanks. Really, I'd rather stay."

Joe struck a pose. "Then I must go, despite the pain," he sang, clutching his chest. "If Fate is kind, we'll meet again."

Woody pushed him toward the door. "If fate is kind you'll choke on a liverwurst sandwich and we'll be able to hire another drummer for this number." He turned back toward Kerry as everyone filed out. "These creeps don't understand an artist needs solitude to create. We'll leave you alone for a half hour, at least."

"Thanks." She stayed in front of the mike until everyone was gone. Then she wandered around the studio. The song was good. Despite her frustration with the recording sessions the past two days, she still believed in its power. But somehow it wasn't transplanting well from a live performance to the hothouse atmosphere of the studio. She wasn't singing it very well, and maybe that was why Tom kept giving it too much of everything—rhythm, echo, vibrato.

She thought of Judd's remark that first day they'd met, when he'd said that love ties could interfere with a budding artist's work. Maybe for some that happened, but for her losing Judd had destroyed her drive. She'd managed last night's performance at the Besotted Fox by tricking herself into believing that a man sitting in the back of the room was Judd. It wasn't, of course, but she'd held on to the fantasy long enough to get through two sets.

But here at the studio she felt his absence like a black hole in her universe. He'd promised her she would forget him in the avalanche of fame soon to come her way. She only needed to get past this first crushing emptiness. She didn't believe him. She wanted him here, now—laughing with her, kissing her, making love to her, bringing out the best she had to give.

A movement in the control booth caught her eye and she glanced up and blinked. Then she shaded her eyes and peered into the dim interior of the booth. Her heartbeat picked up speed. He was there, dressed in a sport shirt and slacks, gazing at her. She feasted on the sight of his topaz eyes, his half smile. Maybe she wanted him so much she'd conjured him up.

Then his voice, darkly resonant, came over the intercom. "I met Tom on the way in. He said you've all been struggling."

"It's me," she said, her throat tight. "I can't—"

"Yes, you can."

"But—"

"Put on your headset. Let's try it without the instruments."

"You're going to record it?"

He gave her a wry smile. "I'm not as good as Billy, but let's try, anyway."

"All right." Adrenaline pumped through her. She had no idea whether she'd be able to control the quality of her voice. But he was still the boss. And it might be her last chance to sing for him. He'd once asked if she could give him passion. Passion he would get.

He sat down and fiddled with the settings on the console. "Tell me when you're ready."

"I'm ready."

"On my signal, then." He held up his hand and closed it into a fist.

She began, and as she sang, the song became a plea. "Shine for me through tempest's wrath, shine for me through blackest night. Show to me the gilded path, and I'll return, beloved light." He was sacrificing what they might have for his daughter's sake, but Rachel would grow up. And Kerry would never stop loving him. At last she admitted to herself the name of the emotion that rocked her each time she thought of him. She loved him, and would go on loving him no matter what happened to her. Fame wouldn't dim her feelings, nor would the long days on the road or the hours spent in a studio.

"But when my soul has drunk its fill, when the tide has lost its pull, then, my love, I'll turn for shore, safe in your arms forevermore." Tears rolled down her cheeks as she gave him the music from her soul. Would he hear the promise she made, and would he believe it?

As she finished, his eyes burned into hers, and for a moment she thought he did believe. Then the light fled from his gaze. "Good," he said, a brusque tone covering what might have been a quiver in his voice.

"Judd, I—"

"You can expect a contract in the mail by the end of the week, along with a copy of this tape. I plan to send you on tour with Saucy Sisters. That means you'll have to be in New York by the first of September, so Tom will have time to pull together a set of more folk tunes and Erica can put some thought into costuming. Can you be here by then?"

She swallowed and brushed at her damp cheeks with the backs of her hands. Her dreams were coming true. She'd done exactly what she'd set out to do. So why did she feel as if she were dying? "Of course," she said. "I'll be here."

15

THE CONTRACT APPEARED in Kerry's mailbox Friday afternoon. The cover letter came from the contracts department, so she didn't even have the small comfort of Judd's signature at the bottom of the letter. Included with the contract was a tape of "The Beacon."

She glanced at the grandfather clock in the hall and made a call to Geoffrey Kent's office. He sounded ready and eager to evaluate the contract for her. She'd have just enough time to run it over and get his opinion before Rachel arrived for her piano lesson.

Geoff greeted her with a smile and a hug. "Big day, huh?"

"I guess it is."

He looked at her more closely. "Not getting cold feet, are you?"

"No," she said quickly. "But the changes I'm facing are finally sinking in. I've lived here all my life, after all."

Geoff nodded. "I understand. But New York's not as far as, say, California, for example."

"Maybe, but when I'm there, I feel a million miles away."

He gave her a sympathetic look. Then he shrugged. "Ah, you'll get over that sooner than you think. You're destined for stardom, Kerry. Not everyone gets a chance at that."

"That's true. I'm pretty lucky."

"And very talented. Have a seat while I take a look at that contract and see if Lighthouse realizes the quality of what they're buying."

Kerry handed Geoff the manila envelope and sat down while he returned to his desk chair and read through the terms.

Finally he glanced up. "Looks more than fair. I knew this day was coming, so I contacted a couple of colleagues who do more of this sort of work than I do. They told me what to look out for, and none of the dangerous clauses are in this." He returned the contract to its envelope and shoved it across the desk toward Kerry. "I'd say it's safe to sign it."

"Thanks, Geoff. If you'll send me a bill, I'll—"

"Absolutely not. This one's on the house. After you start making some of that money they're promising you and you run into legal hassles, then we'll discuss fees. But not today. I'm honored you came to me for advice."

Kerry's eyes unexpectedly filled. "That's what I mean about leaving," she said, blinking back the tears. "Everyone has been so wonderful. Big cities just aren't like that, and I'm really going to miss . . . everything."

"Then you'll have to make lots of trips back here," Geoff said gently. "But don't let a little homesickness cheat you out of the chance of a lifetime."

"That would be pretty stupid, wouldn't it?" Kerry stood and held out her hand. "Thanks, and say hi to Marion for me."

She left Geoff's office and hurried home. Now that she knew the contract was okay she was anxious to listen to the tape. She might be able to manage that before Rachel arrived.

Back in her familiar music room she pushed the Power button on her compact stereo and inserted the tape. She had no idea how she'd sound, considering the emotions she'd felt as she sang it for Judd in the studio, but at least she'd sung the song with passion. Nobody could accuse her of lacking that.

When the tape began with synthesizer music, she frowned. Tom and Billy must have overdubbed the instrumental, although she'd thought from Judd's comment that the tape would stand without it. The synthesizer was too schmaltzy for her taste, but Tom must have known what he was doing.

With the first words of the song, however, she wondered if Tom had a clue. Her voice had an echo and vibrato that hadn't been there when she recorded the song for Judd. What had they done to her voice?

The tape got worse. Strange rhythms appeared, and a disembodied voice chanted, "Come ba-ack, come ba-ack." Kerry stared at the tape deck in consternation. She'd sung an unadulterated version of the song, but it hadn't stayed that way. She'd planned to play the tape when the Honeymooners rehearsed tonight for a wedding reception scheduled tomorrow. They'd begged her to sing the song for them, but she'd held off, believing the tape she'd made for Judd was better than anything she could do again. But it was ruined. She wouldn't play this for anyone.

She rewound the tape and played it again, wondering if she'd overreacted. The second time through was even worse. She felt as if something sacred to her had been violated. If this was the way Lighthouse Records wanted the song to sound, wanted *her* to sound, for that matter, she had some serious thinking to do.

The past four days had been hectic, which had helped her stave off thoughts of Judd. Once she'd told her mother, Aunt June and the band members about the forthcoming contract, word had spread through Eternity with supersonic speed. Her afternoon piano students treated her with such awe they made her chuckle, and a choir rehearsal at the First Congregational church Thursday night had turned into a farce as Louis Bertrand kept rolling an imaginary red carpet around in front of her all night.

But this afternoon, when she gave Rachel her piano lesson, memories of Judd came crashing back. As Kerry put the contract and tape into a desk drawer, she thought what a good thing it was that she and Rachel had formed a relationship before Kerry had even met Judd. That early friendship would prevent Kerry from viewing Rachel simply as an obstacle to her happiness.

Rachel arrived promptly at three, as she had all summer. Kerry opened the door, expecting Rachel to burst into the house as usual, full of excitement. She of all people should be proud of Kerry's new career, since her father was the one making it possible. But, instead of smiles and laughter, Rachel gave her only silence and a grim expression. Kerry recognized that expression. She'd seen it most recently on Judd.

Kerry's first thought made her heart hammer. Somehow Rachel had found out that Kerry and Judd had been lovers in New York. But Rachel couldn't know that unless Judd had told her, and telling his daughter such a thing wouldn't make any sense.

Rachel plopped down on the piano bench and stared at the grand piano's keys as if she'd never seen them before.

"Have you had much chance to practice this week?" Kerry sat in the Queen Anne chair positioned to the right of the keyboard, a lesson-plan book in her lap.

Rachel shook her head.

"I guess you heard the news about my contract."

Rachel glanced up and attempted a smile. "Yeah. That's great, Kerry."

Kerry had never seen the girl so down. Even her skin seemed to have lost some of its color, and the freckles across her nose stood out more prominently. Her sun-bleached hair was woven into an intricate French braid. Normally it would be coming loose by this time of day, but the braid looked perfect.

"Shall we start with some scales?" Kerry was almost afraid to ask Rachel what was wrong for fear that somehow Judd had let something slip. Maybe he'd inadvertently mentioned that Kerry had stayed in the apartment with him. That might trouble someone Rachel's age.

Rachel obediently began the measured stair-climbing rhythm of the scales. Usually she complained about doing them and pulled grotesque faces that made Kerry laugh. Today Rachel played her scales like a trained monkey, without any expression on her face.

Finally Kerry couldn't stand another minute of the tension. "Something is terribly wrong, Rachel."

The girl stopped playing and looked at her. "Did I miss a note? I thought I played them all."

"You played perfectly. I only meant that you seem very depressed today. I've never seen you look so gloomy."

Rachel mumbled something unintelligible.

"Excuse me? I couldn't hear you."

She raised her voice. "I said my dad doesn't want me."

"What?" Kerry made a grab for the lesson-plan book that had slipped from her lifeless fingers. "Rachel, that can't be right!"

"Then why is he making me live with Grandpa and Grandma from now on?"

Kerry clutched the lesson book to her chest. "He is?"

Rachel nodded. "He was here Sunday and he told me about it. He just said, 'Well, punkin, I think you'd be better off staying down here and going to school, don't you?'"

A wave of hot anger washed over Kerry. So he couldn't make a commitment because of his daughter? Wasn't that the line he'd handed her Friday night? "And what did you say?"

"I started to say no, and then Grandma said we'd have so much fun, and she hugged me. I looked at my dad, trying to tell what he was thinking, and his eyes looked kind of stony, you know?"

"Yes." Did she ever.

"So then I thought he wanted to get rid of me. You know I'm not really his daughter. I'm adopted."

"You are so his daughter!" Kerry moved to the piano bench and put both arms around the girl. "He loves you more than anything, Rachel."

"Then why wouldn't he want me to stay in New York with him?" Her young voice was beginning to crack from the effort not to cry. "I know he has a lot of work to do, but I can be really quiet when I have to. This summer was okay, except I missed him a lot, but I kept thinking we'd be back in New York soon, and he'd be able to give me a good-night hug again, and sing me those songs he played when he was in a band, and have paper airplane contests, and...and..." Rachel lost the fight and began to cry.

"Oh, Rachel." Kerry held her close and rocked back and forth. "I really don't understand. This is crazy." Her tone was soothing, but underneath she was boiling with rage. How dared he? Within two days of telling Kerry that Rachel required all his free time, he'd pawned her off on her grandparents. He couldn't have done it to pave the way for his relationship with Kerry, because he would have contacted her by now. Besides, she never would have approved such a move, even if it meant she and Judd could be together.

Had she so completely misread him? Was he a sexual opportunist who bedded hopeful young artists on their way to the top and discarded them before things got too sticky? Had she given her heart to a complete louse?

Kerry couldn't believe it, but the evidence didn't look good. She couldn't voice her opinions to Rachel, who needed to believe in a noble, kind father, even if he wasn't acting that way. As she rocked the sobbing little girl, she knew one thing—Judd had made a horrible mess of his dealings with two people he'd claimed to care for. That alone was enough to make her want to have him keelhauled.

Rachel's sobs softened to jerky whimpers, and Kerry reached into her pocket for a tissue. "I don't think we'll be having a piano lesson today," she said, handing Rachel the tissue. "But I have a better idea, something I like to do when I'm upset."

"Wh-what's that?" Rachel blew her nose vigorously.

"My family has a little sailboat. Taking it out always seems to blow my troubles away. Want to come sailing with me?"

Rachel hesitated for only a moment. "Sure," she said, with a firm nod of her head. She blew her nose again and handed the tissue to Kerry. Kerry suppressed a smile and tucked the soggy tissue into her pocket. That was one reason she loved her young piano students. They hadn't mastered all the social niceties yet, which made them all the more endearing. Signing the contract upstairs would end her teaching days forever, she suddenly realized with an unwelcome pang of regret.

She stood. "If you'll wait here, I'll change into shorts. Maybe you should call your grandparents and tell them where we'll be."

"They might not be there. I think they were going out clamming for a while."

"Then just leave a message on their answering machine. We'll be back before five."

"Can I have a doughnut before we leave?"

Kerry smiled. Rachel was recovering if she could think about doughnuts. "We'll each take one and eat it on the way."

Moments later they turned onto Wharf Street, biting into the soft doughnuts and licking sugar and cinnamon from their fingers.

"Kerry!"

She turned and saw Brent Powell emerging from the restaurant. "Has the contract come yet?" he called.

"Just got it today," Kerry called back.

"And the tape?"

"Uh, yeah."

"Great. Let me know when I can hear it."

Never, Kerry thought. Some accident would have to befall that tape. Maybe she'd spill coffee on it.

"What tape is he talking about?" Rachel asked, skipping along next to her.

"One I made in New York. It's not that good, to tell you the truth."

"I bet you're just saying that. I bet it's wonderful, just like everything you sing. And Lighthouse does very nice work."

This last statement was delivered in such an adult tone Kerry had to suppress a laugh. "Yes, it does," she agreed, thinking that was the best course to take. Rachel was such an interesting combination of child and grown-up. She'd lived in the world of adults so much that she'd picked up their patterns of speech, but in other things, such as her passion for cinnamon doughnuts, she was all kid.

"Did you like New York?" Rachel asked.

Did she? She wondered if she could separate her memories of New York from her memories of Judd. Probably not. But she tried and came up with images of battling for a taxi, sweltering in a crowd of people sandwiched between buildings that blocked the breeze, and breathing in car exhaust. "Central Park was nice," she said at last.

"I *love* Central Park. We live right across from it, you know."

Yes, I know. "Is that right? What a great place to live." Then she could have bitten her tongue, because Rachel's face clouded.

"It was," she said in a forlorn voice.

Kerry's heart wrenched and her anger at Judd grew. Why was he tearing this child's world apart? But she could do little more than comfort Rachel, since she was afraid that Judd's intentions might be entirely selfish. Kerry put an arm around Rachel's shoulders. "Ever been sailing before?"

"Nope."

"Actually, there's not much wind. We might have to use the motor and just chug around for a while. But that's fun, too." They reached the steps leading down to the weathered gray dock.

"I always wanted to go."

Kerry surveyed the few vessels moored there. The charter fishing boats were still out, and many of the sailboats were out, too, despite the lack of wind. "I guess your grandparents don't have a boat, then."

"No."

As they passed a mooring post, the gull sitting on it cocked his head at them but didn't move. "I couldn't afford one all by myself, so I'm glad our family shares this one. Sometimes my brothers and sisters come down and take it out, but mostly I'm the one who uses it."

Rachel wrinkled her nose. "Smells kind of fishy around here."

"I know. I love that smell."

"You do?"

"Sure. My dad was a fisherman. The most fun thing in the world was going out on his boat. Well, here we are." The *Leprechaun II* bobbed gently next to the dock.

"It's cute."

"We bought it secondhand one summer after we decided the Muldoons had always owned boats and we shouldn't break the tradition. Besides, our dad taught us all to sail, and my brothers and sisters wanted to teach their kids."

Rachel peered at the name and Roman numeral stenciled on the stern. "The *Leprechaun II*," she read. "Was there a number one?"

"My dad's old fishing boat, the one Mom had to sell when he died."

"Did he drown?"

Kerry thought of Rachel's parents. Of course she'd assume that. "No. He caught a bad cold that turned into pneumonia. He hated doctors, so by the time he went to one, it was too late."

"How old were you?"

"Eleven."

Rachel studied her. "I barely remember my mom and dad. Well, I call him my dad, but Judd's really my dad now. Still I used to wish I could remember better, wish I'd been older." She gazed at Kerry. "Maybe that wouldn't be so good, either."

"Oh, Rachel." Kerry hugged her. "Everything will be okay."

"I hope so."

Kerry gave her another squeeze. "Now let's get out on that water and blow all our troubles away. What do you say?"

"Yeah, let's."

"You stay here on the dock and I'll get the engine started. I don't think we'll bother with the sails, if you don't mind." She glanced at the bright blue coverings that sheathed the furled sails. "It's frustrating to try and sail with no wind."

"If we don't use the sails this time, can we do it next time?"

"Sure, we . . ." Then Kerry wondered if there would be a next time. Her days on the water were numbered. "We'll try," she amended, disappointed that she couldn't promise. The idea of teaching Rachel to sail appealed to her. She'd never thought in terms of passing along her knowledge, but now she understood why her brothers and sisters were so insistent about the boat and the idea of raising another generation of sailors.

She hopped onto the deck and felt the surge of excitement at the slight roll under her feet. She rummaged in a locker and found two faded orange life vests, one adult and one child-size. She handed one up to Rachel and put the other on. "This is the first rule on the *Leprechaun*," she said, repeating a line her father had used. "Nobody rides without a life jacket."

The motor started easily. Her brothers had tinkered with it when they were down over the Fourth of July. Kerry glanced back to where Rachel stood, her life jacket strapped on, her face aglow with anticipation. "See those two lines looped around the moorings?" she directed. "Lift those off."

Rachel struggled a little with the task, but she managed. Kerry realized Rachel was almost the same age she herself had been when she took her first trip alone with her father. She could pretend she was carrying on the tradition with Rachel.

"Now, be very careful and hop down to the deck," Kerry said, holding the chugging boat as steady as possible. The leap was pretty easy, compared to the one she'd had to make to get onto her father's much larger fishing boat. But she watched Rachel's every movement, aware of her responsibility for the child's safety.

Rachel jumped like a pro and grinned at Kerry. "Anchors aweigh!"

"You bet, sailor." She steered out into the river channel, waving at passing boats as she pointed the prow of the *Leprechaun* toward the open sea.

Rachel stood beside her, her earlier pallor gone. "This is neat."

"Sure is." Kerry took a deep breath of the salty air. She should have done this earlier in the week, but there had been so much to do, so many people to talk with, wedding receptions to play for, replacement singers to interview. She had to train one of the guys to handle the bookings from now on, and none of them much wanted the job. She hadn't realized how the stress was affecting her until now, when the knots in her stomach loosened with the gentle movement of the boat's prow through the water.

She came to the mouth of the river and increased speed a little. Her hair lifted back and away from her face. She glanced at Rachel, who leaned forward and smiled. The breeze created by their movement was teasing her hair out of its careful braid. "Your hair will come undone," Kerry warned. "You can sit down on the deck where it's less windy, if you—"

"Are you kidding? I *love* this," Rachel said, lifting her chin. "If I had a boat like this, I'd be out in it all the time."

"Not in the winter, you wouldn't," Kerry said. "My dad used to, because it was his job, but I'm too much of a wimp to come out here then. One of my brothers always comes down in October, and we put the *Leprechaun* in dry dock."

"And take it out in the spring?"

"Right. We make a party of it, and everybody who's free comes down to help paint and get it ready for the season."

"Sounds like fun."

"It is. I usually pester my brothers to get the boat ready earlier and earlier every year." Kerry's reminiscing came to a halt as she realized that she wouldn't be here in October to take the boat out of the water, nor was she likely to be around in the spring when the boat was repainted and returned to the water.

Rachel turned around and looked back at the town. "Eternity looks like a diorama I made once for school," she said. "And there's the lighthouse. Can we go down that way?"

Kerry obediently turned the *Leprechaun*'s prow in that direction. Her life seemed to be circumvented by lighthouses these days, but she liked this route, too. She liked lighthouses, as a matter of fact. When she'd heard why Judd had renamed his record company, she'd liked them even better.

Rachel slipped her arm around Kerry's waist. "Thanks for taking me for a boat ride," she said, glancing up shyly through her lashes.

Kerry hugged her with her free hand. "My extreme pleasure." She couldn't imagine why Judd would send this girl away. If Rachel were Kerry's daughter, she'd cherish every moment spent with her.

JUDD WASN'T SATISFIED with the way Rachel had taken his decision that she move permanently to her grand-parents' house. He'd expected some resistance, but he'd planned to stay firm. He thought that once Rachel got used to the idea, she'd be fine. He hadn't thought it would take more than a couple of days, and surely she'd be acclimated to the idea by the end of the week.

But when he phoned this morning Rachel had sounded distant and unhappy. He hadn't meant to drive to Eternity this weekend; work was really piling up after Kerry had played havoc with his schedule and concentration the week before. But he had to make sure Rachel was adjusting to the idea of living in Eternity.

He'd also decided she'd feel better with more of her things with her, so he'd loaded the car with some of her favorite stuffed animals, a few games and some warmer clothes for school. Ignoring the stack of messages on his desk, he'd left the office early and driven up to Massachusetts to surprise her.

When no one answered the door at the Woodhouses, he figured they might have gone for a drive, or even out to dinner. Maybe that was better. He had his own key, and now he'd have time to unload the stuff and arrange it in Rachel's room. As he'd packed the car he'd kept a tight lid on his emotions. In fact, he'd been doing that ever since he'd left Kerry on Saturday. He couldn't allow his own selfish feelings to screw up the lives of two people who meant the world to him.

With a koala bear and a skunk under one arm, he let himself in the front door. After taking the stuffed animals up to Rachel's vibrantly colored room, he came downstairs and had started out the door when he noticed a note on the hall table:

Rachel—Grandpa and I should be back from clamming before five, but if we're a little late, you can have a few of the bing cherries if you're hungry.

Love, Grandma

Judd glanced at his watch. It was nearly five. Rachel walked to her piano lesson and back, but even factoring in her time doing that, she should be home by now. He felt a flash of concern that Stella and Allen weren't here, waiting for her, but he told himself that was because he thought like a New Yorker, not like a resident of Eternity. Rachel was almost ten. She could handle being alone for less than an hour, considering that a lot of people in Eternity didn't even lock their doors.

Still, Rachel ought to be here by now. Maybe he should check the answering machine, in case she'd called.

The red light was blinking, and he pushed the button to hear the single message. Sure enough, Rachel's voice was on the recording:

"Hi, Grandma and Grandpa. Rachel's taking me for a ride in her sailboat. I know Daddy doesn't want me on boats, but I didn't think you and Grandpa would mind, and I guess you're in charge of me now. Kerry says we'll be back around five. Bye."

16

KERRY AND RACHEL were laughing over the antics of a gull who seemed determined they had food for him. The gull followed them upriver, squawking in protest as they drew closer to the dock and he still hadn't been fed.

"Don't we have *anything* to throw to him?" Rachel asked.

"He's tough out of luck," Kerry said with a chuckle.

"Well, next time I'm gonna— Uh-oh."

"What?" A smile still on her face, Kerry looked down at Rachel.

"There's Dad."

Kerry glanced at the dock and saw him standing there, feet apart, fists on his hips, his back as stiff as the mast jutting upward from the *Leprechaun*. He looked threatening. And exciting. Her heart skipped into a faster rhythm. "What's he doing here?"

"I don't know, but he's gonna be mad."

"Why?"

"He's never let me go out on a boat before."

Kerry's mouth went dry. "Why not?" But she knew the reason. It was illogical, but she could imagine the way Judd might think after what had happened to Rachel's parents.

"He doesn't want me to get drowned," Rachel explained unnecessarily.

"Well, you didn't." She veered the boat around to back it into the slip. She was good at docking a boat, but her hands shook and she had to make two tries. The whole time she was aware of Judd maintaining that imposing stance, glaring at the *Leprechaun* as if he'd like to snatch it and its occupants from the water with his bare hands.

"Throw your father the mooring lines," she said to Rachel as she eased the boat into position. "As long as he's here, he may as well help."

"Here, Dad. Catch," Rachel said, tossing him a line.

Kerry glanced over her shoulder and saw his expert catch, his catlike grace as he secured the boat. Zorba had obviously taught him well. She wished Zorba had also convinced him not to blame the sea for taking his brother's life. Rachel was a natural sailor, and if he insisted on keeping her away from boats . . . But who was he to insist on anything? Her earlier anger returned, redoubled by this new evidence of Judd's arrogance. He was sending Rachel away, yet he claimed the right to dictate her life from afar. Just who the hell did he think he was?

By the time she'd turned off the motor and removed her life jacket, she was ready for battle. She stowed her life jacket and Rachel's in the storage locker, her hands shaking with rage. Judd coaxed people to love him—Rachel, and then her—but he didn't have any staying power, no backbone for the long haul. Kerry's need to protect Rachel overrode any concern for her own emotional well-being. Judd had to be set straight.

Judd helped Rachel up to the dock and turned to offer Kerry his hand. She ignored it, put her hand on the stern of the *Leprechaun* and vaulted smoothly to the dock.

"Now that you're both safely on land—" Judd began.

"Don't even start." Kerry stepped forward and lifted her chin in defiance. "I know just what you're going to say, and you can save your breath. Because if what Rachel tells me is true and you're shipping her down here permanently, you'd better give up this idiotic notion about keeping her off boats."

"I don't want her out on the water!" His topaz eyes blazed, leonine and imperious.

"She's a born sailor. You have no right to keep her from an environment she fits into perfectly. *Especially* if you're going to dangle the ocean and boats in front of her nose while you live your swinging bachelor existence in New York!"

His jaw clenched. "I'm not living—" He threw his hands in the air and spun away from her. "Why am I explaining anything to you? This is none of your concern."

She'd heard that love and hate were two sides of the same coin. Now she understood. "The hell it isn't! Sorry, Rachel. Would you like to walk up the dock a ways so your father and I can fight?"

"I want to listen." She stood, eyes wide, glancing from Judd's face to Kerry's.

"Rachel, take a hike," Judd said.

"I never get in on *anything*." Head down, Rachel scuffed along to the foot of the dock.

"All right, Judd Roarke." Kerry faced him, her feet planted apart as his had been. "You told me we couldn't have a relationship because your spare time belonged to that wonderful girl down there. So what's this latest idiocy?"

His tone was low and ominous. "As I said, it's not your concern."

"If you mean the part where you lied to me about your priorities, I guess you're right. It's a creative way to dump an unwanted element in your life, but if you want to use Rachel as an excuse to get rid of me, that's your problem."

"I told you the truth, dammit!"

"Ah, but now the truth has changed a bit, hasn't it?"

"I don't want to discuss this with you. Rachel and I are going home now." He turned to leave.

"To which home, Judd? Fact is, she doesn't believe she has one anymore."

He paused.

"That's right. She thinks the reason you're pushing her to live in Eternity is that you don't want her anymore."

"She can't think that." His voice had a note of anguish she hadn't heard before.

"She can think anything she wants, Judd. She's an individual, with a right to her own thoughts. She told me some of them this afternoon. I don't know what your twisted reasons for your decision to have her live here are, but you're breaking her heart."

"She doesn't understand what's best—"

"For her? Or for you?"

"For God's sake, she's only nine!"

"That's old enough to understand rejection," Kerry said quietly.

"Oh, *hell*." Judd whirled away from her and strode toward the foot of the dock. When he reached Rachel, he put an arm around her shoulders and led her to his car, parked next to the landing.

Kerry watched them drive away, her vision blurred with tears. She also understood rejection, and it hurt more than she thought she could bear.

RATHER THAN PLAY the tape of her song for anyone in town, Rachel decided to teach it to the First Congregational church choir and have them perform it on Sunday morning. She called a special rehearsal for Saturday afternoon and within an hour the group had it. Sure, the rendition had its flaws. Patience Powell, Aunt June's sister, always pitched her voice an octave above everyone else, and she didn't carry the tune with much skill. Louis Bertrand kept forgetting the words because he was too busy winking at whatever woman happened to catch his eye.

Overall, though, Kerry was satisfied with the results. She liked the church choir's version a heck of a lot better than the one that had come out of Lighthouse's studio. And the choir members loved the song. They made her tell them the story of the nanny in Central Park at least four times.

"It's a love song, of course," Louis, the old roué, said slyly.

"Yes," Kerry said, "but I thought it would still be appropriate to sing it in church. There's an almost spiritual quality to it."

"I thoroughly agree," said Aunt June. "And what better way to introduce the song to lots of people. If word of it gets out," she added with a look that promised word would definitely get out, "we're liable to draw from some of the other congregations in town."

"What a great idea," Aunt Patience said.

Aunt June glanced at Kerry. "I heard Judd Roarke is in town again this weekend. Is he here to pick up the signed contract from you?"

"I hardly think he'd make a trip up here just for that," Kerry said. She hadn't signed the contract yet. She would, of course.

"Dan Murphy said he saw you talking to Judd on the landing yesterday afternoon," Dodie Gibson said. She smiled. "High-level negotiations, Kerry? Holding out for more money?"

"No." Kerry realized with a jolt that she hadn't even looked at the money offered in the contract. She had no idea how much Lighthouse Records was prepared to pay her. "I took Rachel out on the boat, and Judd came down to meet us." Did he ever. That scene had ended whatever hopes she'd secretly nurtured of rebuilding a relationship. He seemed determined to sever all connections with her.

Emma Webster cleared her throat. "I think we should celebrate Kerry's success. With Judd Roarke in town, we could make both of them the guests of honor. Maybe we could throw something together tonight, or early tomorrow, after church services. We have enough people here right now to organize it."

Kerry panicked. "Oh, that's not necessary. Tonight wouldn't work, anyway, because we have the Payson-Dibble wedding, and the Honeymooners are playing for the reception afterward, which could last until late. And I'm sure Judd will be leaving early tomorrow."

"It wouldn't hurt to ask," Dodie said. "I wouldn't mind being the one to do it, either."

Kerry scrambled for another excuse. "It's really hot this weekend. Maybe later, when it cools off, we could—"

"Nonsense," Emma said. "It's no hotter than usual for this time of year. We'll just have plenty of iced tea and lemonade. We could set up tables on Soldier's Green, make it a giant potluck. I think the town wants this, Kerry. We're all very proud of you. Let us have a little fun."

Kerry swallowed. There seemed no way out of it. Judd probably wouldn't come, so what harm was there in letting the town enjoy this moment of triumph? People had been waiting a long time to see her make good. "All right," she said. "I guess after church to-morrow is okay."

KERRY HAD ASKED for her song to be the final part of the church program the next morning, and as the moment came, her excitement grew.

At last Pastor Bue gave her a nod. The song was mentioned in the morning's printed program, so Kerry had decided not to introduce it. She turned to her choir, blew her pitch pipe and raised her hands. The choir would sing without accompaniment. She prayed they'd stay in tune, although that wasn't usually their strong point, but she didn't want the sound of the organ to interfere with the lyrics. She'd never seen the choir members look as expectant as they did now.

From the moment the first notes of the song filled the historic church, Kerry felt a tingling up her spine. Yes, this was right. Patience shot up an octave, as usual, but for some reason, with this song, it sounded good. For once Louis Bertrand watched Kerry's direction, instead of the ladies he was trying to flirt with, and Dodie Gibson's lovely contralto came through with a richness Kerry had never heard before. Tears pushed at her eyes, and her throat tightened. This song didn't belong on the pop circuit.

It belonged to Eternity.

By the time the song ended, tears were streaming down her cheeks and dampening the faces of the choir. A long silence followed the end of the song. She smiled mistily at the choir, then turned to the congregation, which broke into applause.

Then everyone was up and rushing toward her, forgetting the usual orderly recession that traditionally ended the service.

Pastor Bue's voice rose above the hubbub. "Time to party!"

Kerry was whisked out the door and across the street to the green on a tide of well-wishers.

Ted Webster and his wife, Ruthie, appeared beside her.

"That song was beautiful," Ted said.

"Thank you," Kerry managed around the lump that was still lodged in her throat.

"We're going to miss you, Kerry," Ruthie said.

Kerry couldn't reply. The tightness wouldn't leave her throat. The song had been so right. Leaving Eternity seemed so wrong.

Soldier's Green was a kaleidoscope of picnic hampers, lawn chairs and people in Sunday dress. It was hot, but no one paid attention except to make sure the potato salad stayed chilled and the ice held out.

Kerry was kept busy talking to everyone. Grubby Daniels shoved a full plate of food at her with an admonition to eat it, but she had no time between accepting congratulations and explaining who the Saucy Sisters were and where she'd go on tour. Just as well she didn't try to eat. She'd didn't feel hungry.

At last, inevitably, someone called for Kerry to make a speech. She tried to duck the issue, but hands divested her of her barely touched plate, shoved her forward and hoisted her on top of a cleared space on a picnic table.

She stood there looking around at the friends and neighbors she'd known all her life, loved all her life. This was her chance to tell them goodbye, to thank them for all the support they'd given her over the years, to promise them she wouldn't forget Eternity and all of them.

She couldn't say the words. Images kept intruding—feeding the gulls, sailing away from the town landing, leading the church choir, painting the *Leprechaun II* with her brothers, coaxing a new piano student, singing for a wedding reception, joking with the Honeymooners.

I just want you to be happy, her father had said. Well, she was.

Then she thought of riding on a cramped tour bus, of days without a moment to herself, of singing a butchered version of the song, of being landlocked somewhere in middle America, far from the ocean, far from gulls, far from Eternity. But if she did what she wanted to do, would the people of Eternity still love her?

And what about Judd? He'd acted like a heel, but he didn't deserve to have his efforts in her behalf thrown back in his face. She opened her mouth, closed it. Opened it again. Cleared her throat.

Everyone waited, faces turned up toward her, smiles on their faces.

"I'm . . . I'm not going."

People frowned in confusion.

"What do you mean, not going?" Aunt June hollered from the middle of the crowd. "Of course you are."

Kerry shook her head. "I'm sorry, Aunt June," she said hoarsely. "I'm sorry, everyone. But that song belongs to Eternity, and so do I."

A chorus of protests and questions rose to engulf her. She shook her head and climbed down from the table.

People reached for her, called her name, but she dodged them and pushed toward the edge of the crowd with mumbled excuses. Finally she gained the street and began to run.

They wouldn't follow her. People in Eternity had been raised with the good manners to leave someone alone if she wanted to be alone. She turned right down School Street and slowed to a fast walk. In the distance she could see the lighthouse, standing like a beacon. She set out for it.

17

JUDD WAS LOADING Rachel's stuffed animals back in the car when she and her grandparents came back from the celebration for Kerry. He hadn't thought Kerry would want to see him there, so he'd politely refused Dodie Gibson's invitation.

Rachel burst from the car as soon as it stopped. "Daddy! Kerry says she's not going to New York!"

He turned, a pink bear in his arms. "What?"

"She was supposed to make this goodbye speech—" Rachel waved her arms in her excitement "—and, instead, she said she wasn't going!"

Judd glanced for confirmation at Stella and Allen, who had climbed out of the car.

"That's right, Judd," Allen said. "Strangest thing I've ever seen. I can't imagine what got into her."

"She said something about the song belonging to Eternity, and so did she," Stella added. "Then she walked away, actually ran away."

"Where?"

He shoved the bear into the back seat and fumbled in his pants pocket for his keys.

"Toward the beach," Rachel said, watching her father. "Are you going after her?"

"I'm going to talk to her."

"Can I go?"

"No, punkin. This is between Kerry and me."

"Don't be mad at her, Daddy."

He noticed she'd reverted from "Dad" to "Daddy," ever since their long talk the night before. He liked the sound of it. "I'm not mad at her, Rachel," he said. "I just don't want her to be mad at herself." He glanced across the top of the car toward Stella and Allen. "I'm not sure how long I'll be."

Stella was watching him with a speculative light in her eyes. "Take your time," she said.

With a short nod he got behind the wheel and backed out of the drive.

His thoughts as he drove to the beach tumbled like small stones rolling in the surf. But one resolution kept bobbing to the surface—if Kerry was doing this either to punish him or avoid working with him, he had to get her back on track. He should never have made love to her. He could have encouraged her without going that far, couldn't he? But no, his hormones had raged out of control, and now perhaps he'd tarnished her dream. He hit the steering wheel in frustration.

As he parked the car he saw her walking far down the beach near the lighthouse. How fitting. He was responsible for her being on the rocks. Could he repair the damage he'd done?

He started down the beach at a jog, getting sand in his loafers with every step. He ignored the gritty feeling and went faster. When he was close enough, he shouted her name.

She turned, saw him and started walking toward him. He was relieved. He'd wondered if he'd have to chase her down and force her to listen to him.

He expected belligerence, anger, all the emotions she'd deservedly thrown at him the other day.

Yet when she drew near she looked at him, her green eyes clear and free of anger, almost luminescent in their calmness. Her hair, blown by the breeze, was in tantalizing disarray. She was so beautiful she made his throat ache.

"I'm sorry, Judd," she said.

He slowed and tried to catch his breath. His heart had been pumping adrenaline into his system ever since Rachel had told him of Kerry's decision. And he sure hadn't expected an apology from her. He tried to get his bearings, tried to ignore the bewitching sight of her standing barefoot in the sand, her shoes dangling from one hand.

"You could sue me for breach of contract, except fortunately I haven't signed anything yet," she continued, gazing at him with a serenity he found unnerving.

"You're doing this because of me, aren't you?"

She smiled. "You really do take responsibility for everything, don't you?"

"If I hadn't loused up your stay in New York . . ."

"You didn't. At least not until last Saturday. I'll never forget the incredible times we had together, Judd, even though we'll never have those times again. You were the best part of New York. The rest doesn't suit me very well."

"You can't know that."

She shoved her hands in the pockets of her full denim skirt. "Did you listen to the tape before the contracts department sent it to me?"

"No." He hadn't been able to, but he couldn't admit that now, not when he needed to be impersonal. "I left the tape editing to Tom and Billy."

"Well, that's something."

He frowned. "What do you mean?"

"If you'd okayed that tape, I'd wonder how you could ever make a success of Lighthouse Records."

"It was bad?"

"Worse than bad."

He frowned impatiently. "Kerry, if you're disappointed with the tape, that can be fixed. If you're disappointed with me, I'll stay out of your way, but don't give up your career because of a rocky start. Go to another recording company if you want. I'll recommend you to several, although you probably don't even need my recommendation."

"I don't want another company. I regret all the time you've wasted on me, Judd. My decision is horribly unprofessional, but then, that's the point, isn't it? I don't want to be a professional."

"Wasn't the money enough? I could—"

"I didn't even look at how much money Lighthouse offered me."

He stared at her. "You're not making sense."

"It's very simple, really. I don't want to be a star."

"But you've wanted that all your life!"

She shook her head slowly. "Other people wanted it for me. I'd been given The Muldoon Gift, and felt a duty to make use of it. And I will, but here in Eternity, doing what I love. I wouldn't be happy out there under the bright lights, Judd. I'd dry up. Except I didn't know that until now. So I have lots of apologies to make—to Aunt June and my mother, to all the people who've cheered me on all these years." She paused and gazed out to sea. "But in the end, it's my life I'll be living, not theirs."

Hope cascaded through him, warming the coldness that had seeped into every pore of his body since Saturday morning. "Are you absolutely sure about this?"

She met his gaze. "Absolutely. Thanks for the chance, Judd. And the good times. They were good, and I don't want to ruin them with recriminations." She held out her hand. "Let's just part friends."

He took her hand. "The hell with that," he muttered, and pulled her into his arms.

She glanced up at him, startled.

"Do you promise me that you know what you're doing, that you won't look back ten years from now and wish you'd chosen differently?"

"I know what I'm doing," she said, color staining her cheeks. "But I'm not at all sure about you."

"How could you know anything about me?" he said, his voice husky. "I've hidden everything from you."

She searched his gaze. Her lips parted slightly, and it took all his control not to kiss her senseless, but he had some things to say. And he might as well begin with the most important.

"I love you," he said, putting all his pent-up emotions into the words. "Madly, passionately and forever."

She let out a long, slow sigh. "Oh," she whispered.

"But I couldn't tell you that and jeopardize your career. I didn't dare ask you to marry me, and love me forever, and be a mother to Rachel, even when those were the only words I wanted to say."

Her green eyes grew dusky with desire. "And now?"

"Now I dare everything." He couldn't hold back a moment longer. Her lips beckoned to him, and he leaned down to taste her, groaning at the sweetness of her mouth. Her response told him what he needed to know.

But suddenly she pulled away, gasping. "We have a problem. You live in New York. As much as I love you, I don't want to live in New York."

"You love me?"

"Of course."

"Then we have no problems." He resumed kissing her.

At last she wrenched her lips away. "Judd, this is important."

"I know. That's why we'll live in Eternity. Rachel loves it here. I'll keep the apartment in New York, and maybe sometimes I'll have to spend a few days there, but there's no reason I can't run the business from here."

"Judd, I've been there. I know how involved . . ."

"I'll be less involved. You jolted me out of that thinking the other day. Before that, I somehow thought I couldn't cut back, so I decided to have Rachel stay with the people who could give her more time. But that's crazy. Of course I can cut back. Who am I working for, if not you and Rachel?" He chuckled. "Rachel told me Friday night she doesn't even want to inherit the record company. She wants to grow up and make movies with Jason Priestly."

"Oh, Judd." She touched his face, and the gentle pressure made him close his eyes in ecstasy. "Did that hurt you—that she doesn't want what you've been building up for her?"

He grasped her hand and pressed his lips against her palm. "Not when I realized that she'd freed me from building it up. I might even sell it."

She grinned. "And play sax for the Honeymooners?"

"Who knows?" He laughed and spun her around. "I just know I love you, Kerry Muldoon, and I want to get married in that confounded chapel and live happily ever after."

"Better be careful. The marriages performed there seem to have real staying power."

"I'm counting on it," he said, and settled his lips over hers once more.

WHEN KERRY'S SISTER Maureen learned that Bruce Springsteen would be the best man opposite her as matron of honor at Kerry and Judd's wedding, Kerry realized it was the first time her sister had been at a loss for words.

Kerry and Judd soon discovered the chapel would never hold his star-studded guest list, coupled with her list, which included nearly everyone in Eternity and old friends from college. They decided to limit the service to immediate family members and the most intimate friends. The rest would be invited to a gigantic reception that Kerry figured would be a media magnet.

She'd have preferred less publicity. But since she'd deprived Eternity of her glory, a celebrity wedding was the least she could provide to boost the town's spirits.

In the days leading up to the wedding, nearly everyone in Eternity had managed to get Kerry aside and tell her they thought she was doing the right thing. Everyone except Aunt June. Kerry had tried to talk with her, but each conversation ended with Aunt June sighing and shaking her head. She didn't say so, but it was obvious she thought Kerry was making a terrible mistake.

Nevertheless, Kerry had invited her to the wedding, and she'd accepted.

The day of the ceremony, the last day of August, the sun beat down as if to warm the hearts of anyone who still felt a trace of disappointment. Clouds white as new sailcloth puffed high in the sky for just a touch of contrast.

Kerry had seen pictures of Nôtre Dame in Paris and St. Peter's in Rome. She'd passed by the majestic St. Patrick's Cathedral in New York. But only the Eternity chapel gave her goose bumps.

Perhaps it was the simplicity, she thought, appreciating anew the rough plaster walls lovingly whitewashed each year, the high narrow windows paned in diamond-shaped leaded glass, the plain yet graceful wooden pews. Perhaps it was the scent of history captured within these walls, or the legacy of freedom represented by the chapel's days as part of the underground railway.

Kerry wore her mother's wedding dress, which had been altered in turn for each of the Muldoon daughters. She was vaguely aware that the introduction to the wedding march had begun and Rachel was starting down the aisle, followed by Maureen, who looked a little faint.

Kerry entered the chapel on the arm of her oldest brother, Sean. The moment they walked in she came alive. Her heart beat wildly as her gaze traveled up the aisle and found Judd, magnificent in a gray morning coat. She saw the well-known face of Springsteen, but her attention immediately returned to Judd. The organist moved into the wedding march, and she started toward him.

In her years with the Honeymooners she'd sung at countless weddings, watched hundreds of brides place their hands trustingly in those of hundreds of grooms. Yet here at the altar with Judd, the world was born again, and no two people had ever stood here with quite so much hope, quite so much joy, quite so much love. She trembled as she looked into his eyes and saw the same awe she felt.

She and Judd repeated the time-honored words as if no one had ever spoken them, slipped a ring on each other's finger as if the tradition began today. And as they gazed into each other's eyes, she sang for him once more, choosing the last verse of "The Beacon," and modifying the words to the shape of what she felt on this glorious wedding day. She felt him tremble as she sang, "Now my love, I've turned for shore, safe in your arms forevermore."

Then, in a heartbeat, they were man and wife, hurrying down the aisle to a wild ovation from family and friends. Zorba, Eternity's newest resident, drove them to the reception, but they could have ridden with King Kong, for all Kerry knew. She was immersed in the depths of topaz eyes.

"I love you more than you'll ever know," Judd murmured, touching her cheek.

"You'll have a long time to try and tell me," she whispered back. "You are good and married, Mr. Roarke."

"That goes for you, too, Mrs. Roarke." He kissed her gently, with a restrained passion that suggested a night ahead neither would ever forget. But first they had a duty to the crowds of people waiting to congratulate them.

They stood close together in the reception line, often touching surreptitiously—brushing hands, elbows, shoulders—as they greeted the famous and the homegrown. The group was an eclectic mix of Fifth Avenue chic and Eternity casual.

At last Aunt June had her turn. She took Kerry's hand and held it firmly in her own. "It came to me," she said.

"What, Aunt June?" Kerry leaned forward, thinking she'd missed something.

"The song. It does belong here. I've heard it before."

Kerry blinked, startled. "You have?"

"Your great-grandmother Muldoon used to sing that song in her old, quavery voice. She insisted on singing it to you when you were a little thing, not more than two. She said somebody had to keep the song going, that it had been sung in Eternity for generations, but now people had forgotten the old songs for the new."

Kerry glanced up at Judd. "Can you believe that?"

His eyes were full of love. "Can I believe you managed to restore that song to the town? You bet."

"What I'm trying to say is," Aunt June continued, gripping her hand tighter, "that you did the right thing."

Tears moistened Kerry's eyes. "Oh, Aunt June."

"You have a gift. We all know that. But only you can choose how to use it. I think you've chosen well."

"Thank you, Aunt June."

"And as for you, young man, I hear you play the saxophone."

Judd choked and had to take a few seconds to clear his throat. "Is that right?" he managed at last.

"I expect to hear you play it soon," Aunt June said. "Talent should not lie idle. We in Eternity don't believe in hiding our lights under bushels."

"I'll keep that in mind, Aunt June."

When she'd moved on down the reception line, Judd leaned over and took a tiny nip at Kerry's ear. "You told," he said in an undertone.

She looked up at him with a sunny smile. "Actually, I discussed it once with Rachel, and she told. But you'd better get used to this sort of thing, Judd. People don't have secrets in Eternity."

"That's what you think."

"Oh?"

"I'm the only one in this entire crowd who knows where we're spending our wedding night."

Grubby Daniels came next in line and hugged Kerry. Then he shook Judd's hand. "The Haven is a perfect wedding-night choice, old buddy," he said with a grin.

Judd groaned as Grubby walked away. "Bet you don't know which room!" he called after him.

Grubby just grinned over his shoulder.

"No privacy," Judd moaned. "None at all."

Kerry laughed and squeezed his hand. "Is that so very important?"

He turned to her with a mischievous gleam in his eye. "Guess not," he said, sweeping her into an embrace. And as the crowd cheered, he kissed the bride.

COMING NEXT MONTH

#505 EVEN COWBOYS GET THE BLUES Carin Rafferty
Lost Loves, Book 5

No *way* would Annie O'Neill ever work with her lying and cheating ex-husband again. So what if Tanner Chapel needed her to help write his country songs? So what if he claimed he wasn't so bad? So what if he was still the sexiest damn cowboy she'd *ever* laid eyes on?

#506 SCANDALS JoAnn Ross

One night of fiery passion changed the lives of Bram Fortune and Dani Cantrell forever. Grieving over the death of Bram's brother, who was also her fiancé, Dani had turned to Bram. Six weeks later Dani learned she was pregnant. Bram insisted they marry...but would Dani ever stop loving his brother?

#507 PLAIN JANE'S MAN Kristine Rolofson

Plain Jane won a man. Well, not *exactly*. Jane Plainfield won a boat and gorgeous Peter Johnson came with it. Jane hated the water, so what was she going to do with the boat? Even worse, she had been badly burned by romance—so what was she going to do with the man? Especially when he wouldn't take *no* for an answer?

#508 STAR Janice Kaiser

Five years ago, Hollywood lured rising star Dina Winters. She landed a movie deal, but left fiancé Michael Cross at the altar. Now hotshot director Michael wants Dina for *his* movie. But she'll need an Oscar-winning performance to work with the sexy man she never stopped loving....

AVAILABLE NOW:

#501 GOLD AND GLITTER
Gina Wilkins
Lost Loves, Book 4

#502 WEDDING SONG
Vicki Lewis Thompson
Weddings, Inc.

#503 THE RANGER MAN
Sheryl Danson

#504 A TRUE BLUE KNIGHT
Roseanne Williams

Where do you find hot Texas nights, smooth Texas charm and dangerously sexy cowboys?

Crystal Creek reverberates with the exciting rhythm of Texas. Each story features the rugged individuals who live and love in the Lone Star state.

"...a series that should hook any romance reader. Outstanding."

—*Rendezvous*

Praise for Margot Dalton's *Even the Nights Are Better*

"...every bit as engrossing as the others. Ms. Dalton wraps you in sentiment...this is a book you don't just read, you feel."

—*Rendezvous*

Praise for Margot Dalton's *New Way To Fly*

"This is a fine and fitting successor to the first ten Crystal Creek books. May they go on forever."

—*Rendezvous*

Don't miss the next book in this exciting series. Look for
NEVER GIVIN' UP ON LOVE by **MARGOT DALTON**

Available in September wherever Harlequin books are sold.

CC-19

HARLEQUIN®

Temptation

Lost Loves

RIGHT MAN...WRONG TIME

Remember that one man who turned your world upside down? Who made you experience all the ecstatic highs of passion and lows of loss and regret. What if you met him again?

You dared to lose your heart once and had it broken. Dare you love again?

JoAnn Ross, Glenda Sanders, Rita Clay Estrada, Gina Wilkins and Carin Rafferty. Find their stories in Lost Loves, Temptation's newest miniseries, running May to September 1994.

In September, experience EVEN COWBOYS GET THE BLUES by Carin Rafferty. A one-night stand had cost country-western hotshot Tanner Chapel plenty. His marriage with Annie was over, his career was on the skids and his dreams had begun to die. He wanted Annie back...but could she learn to love and trust again?

What if...?

LOST5

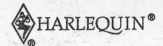

THE WEDDING GAMBLE
Muriel Jensen

Eternity, Massachusetts, was America's wedding town. Paul Bertrand knew this better than anyone—he never should have gotten soused at his friend's rowdy bachelor party. Next morning when he woke up, he found he'd somehow managed to say "I do"—to the woman he'd once jilted! And Christina Bowman had helped launch so many honeymoons, she knew just what to do on theirs!

THE WEDDING GAMBLE, available in September from American Romance, is the fourth book in Harlequin's new cross-line series, **WEDDINGS, INC.**

Be sure to look for the fifth book, **THE VENGEFUL GROOM,** by Sara Wood (Harlequin Presents #1692), coming in October.

WED4

New York Times Bestselling Author

BARBARA DELINSKY

**Look for her at your favorite retail outlet this
September with**

A SINGLE ROSE

A two-week Caribbean treasure hunt with rugged and
sexy Noah VanBaar wasn't Shaye Burke's usual style.
Stuck with Noah on a beat-up old sloop with no engine,
she was left feeling both challenged and confused. Torn
between passion and self-control, Shaye was afraid of
being swept away by an all-consuming love.

Available in September, wherever Harlequin books are sold.

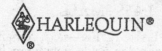 HARLEQUIN®

BD2

This September, discover the fun of falling in love with...

Harlequin is pleased to bring you this exciting new collection of three original short stories by bestselling authors!

ELISE TITLE
BARBARA BRETTON
LASS SMALL

LOVE AND LAUGHTER—sexy, romantic, fun stories guaranteed to tickle your funny bone and fuel your fantasies!

Available in September wherever
Harlequin books are sold.

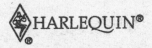

HARLEQUIN®

LOVEL

Fifty red-blooded, white-hot, true-blue hunks
from every State in the Union!

Look for MEN MADE IN AMERICA! Written by some of
our most popular authors, these stories feature fifty of
the strongest, sexiest men, each from a different state in
the union!

Two titles available every month at your favorite retail
outlet.

In August, look for:

PROS AND CONS by Bethany Campbell
(Massachusetts)
TO TAME A WOLF by Anne McAllister (Michigan)

In September, look for:

WINTER LADY by Janet Joyce (Minnesota)
AFTER THE STORM by Rebecca Flanders (Mississippi)

You won't be able to resist MEN MADE IN AMERICA!

If you missed your state or would like to order any other states that have already been
published, send your name, address, zip or postal code along with a check or money
order (please do not send cash) in U.S. for $3.59 plus 75¢ postage and handling for
each book, and in Canada for $3.99 plus $1.00 postage and handling for each book,
payable to Harlequin Reader Service, to:

In the U.S.	In Canada
3010 Walden Avenue	P.O. Box 609
P.O. Box 1369	Fort Erie, Ontario
Buffalo, NY 14269-1369	L2A 5X3

Please specify book title(s) with your order.
Canadian residents add applicable federal and provincial taxes.

MEN894

HARLEQUIN®

Weddings, Inc.

Harlequin Books requests the pleasure of your company this June in Eternity, Massachusetts, for WEDDINGS, INC.

For generations, couples have been coming to Eternity, Massachusetts, to exchange wedding vows. Legend has it that those married in Eternity's chapel are destined for a lifetime of happiness. And the residents are more than willing to give the legend a hand.

Beginning in June, you can experience the legend of Eternity. Watch for one title per month, across all of the Harlequin series.

HARLEQUIN BOOKS... NOT THE SAME OLD STORY!

WEDGEN